Lucy Clark loves movies. She loves binge-watching box-sets of TV shows. She loves reading and she loves to bake. Writing is such an integral part of Lucy's inner being that she often dreams in Technicolor®, waking up in the morning and frantically trying to write down as much as she can remember. You can find Lucy on Facebook and Twitter. Stop by and say g'day!

ONE WEEK TO
WIN HIS HEART

LUCY CLARK

MILLS & BOON

Miss Melanie Mischief Maker—how are you 21?!!
Love you to Voyager and back.

Pr 20:7

CHAPTER ONE

DR MELODY JANEWAY brushed her hands apprehensively down her calf-length blue skirt and ensured her embroidered white blouse was tucked neatly into the waistband. Next, she smoothed a hand over her unruly auburn curls, ensuring her hair was still secured in the clip at the nape of her neck. She was ready to meet the dignitary.

Melody started to pace in front of her desk, taking deep breaths. 'Cool, calm and collected.' She whispered her mantra in an effort to calm her nerves. When the intercom on her desk buzzed, she almost hit the roof with fright. She pressed the button. 'Yes, Rick?'

'The delegation is here.'

'Show them in, thank you.' She closed her eyes for a millisecond. How had she ever let herself be talked into this job? Acting head of the orthopaedic department? It was ridiculous. Not that she minded the administrative side, but many other aspects of the job, such as lecturing and playing host to delegates, weren't her cup of tea. She was a doctor, not a tour guide!

Melody opened her eyes at the sound of her office door opening. Should she be sitting behind her desk? Would that look more official? Oh, well. It was too late to move so instead she stood like a statue in the middle of the large office with a fake smile pasted onto her face.

The smile, however, became genuine when she found

herself staring up at a man with the most gorgeous brown eyes she'd ever seen. He was tall—a lot taller than she'd expected. Probably about six feet three inches. His hair was a rich dark brown, militarily short and starting to grey at the temples.

'I'm George Wilmont.' He extended his hand as he walked towards her.

'Welcome, Professor Wilmont.' She quickly recovered her composure, pleased with herself for not openly gaping at the man. 'I'm Melody Janeway.' She placed her hand in his, the touch sending a jolt of electrifying tingles up her arm. His fingers gripped her hand firmly, warming not only her hand but the rest of her as well.

She'd been unprepared for such a reaction to this stranger, especially as he held her hand for a fraction of a second longer than was necessary. Melody felt something wild and untamed pass between them. His gaze locked with hers and she saw a flicker of surprise register in his eyes before they both dropped their hands and took a small step backwards.

Whoa! What on earth was that? According to the dossier she had on him as part of the preparation information for this tour, he was a married man. Melody cleared her throat, desperately trying to regain her composure. 'Uh… welcome to St Aloysius Hospital, Professor Wilmont.'

He cleared his throat. 'Please, call me George.'

She nodded. 'I'm Melody, and if you want to make any jokes about singing or asking if I can carry a tune, the answer is yes. I sing very well and often in key.'

George smiled at her attempt at humour, a real smile, not a polite *I'm a professional* type of smile. The effect was real as she noted his eyes spark with a glint of merriment. They stared at each other for what seemed like an eternity, the hours ticking by, yet in reality it was no more than five seconds. Still, it was enough to make her feel highly self-conscious. The smile slid from George's lips and he shifted back again, as though needing to put even more distance between them.

'Melody Janeway, allow me to introduce you to the rest of my staff.' George introduced the people who were responsible for helping him keep to the strict timetable he lived by. As a visiting orthopaedic surgeon, George had been touring the world for almost twelve months and had now returned to his homeland of Australia. He had two administrative assistants, one research assistant, one technical consultant and a personal aide.

Melody's own PA, Rick, was hovering by the door. She beckoned him in and introduced him. 'Rick and I are both at your service this week. If there's anything you need to know or can't find, please don't hesitate to ask.' Melody addressed the group as she spoke but her gaze kept returning to George.

'Thank you,' he responded, smiling politely as their gazes held once more. Melody gave herself a mental shake and checked her watch. 'I guess we should make a start. Have there been any changes to the agreed agenda?'

For the past few months, information had been emailed back and forth between Professor Wilmont's organisers and Rick, ensuring operating theatres and lecture halls were booked, as well as confirming catering arrangements and restaurant reservations. Throughout this week, Melody's job was to be the official representative for St Aloysius Hospital, to be the master of ceremonies at some events, or to simply be there to field questions and introduce Professor Wilmont where necessary. It would be a long, arduous week and if there had been any changes to the agenda, it was best to find out now, rather than at the last minute.

Professor Wilmont's delegation had been organising these types of events in hospitals around the globe since the beginning of the tour in January, so they were very experienced at what they did. That was another reason why it was important for Melody and Rick to ensure St Aloysius measured up to the standards of professionalism the professor would have received from other medical institutions.

'Not that I'm aware of.' George answered Melody's question but turned and raised an inquisitive eyebrow at his personal aide. 'Carmel? Any changes?'

Carmel consulted the leather-bound book in her hands, then shook her head. 'No.' She was a small, thin woman who wore very high-heeled shoes and a tailored business suit, with her almost jet-black hair pulled back in a tight chignon. The consummate professional.

'Excellent.' Melody nodded. 'Well, then, we'd better get started to make sure we don't fall behind schedule.'

'Carmel would never let that happen,' George remarked as Melody walked towards the door and held it open. 'She's a hard taskmaster but a necessary one.' His words were spoken with affection and joviality. Carmel's answer was to provide a polite smile in their direction. 'I'd have been lost without her during this tour.'

George was the last person to exit, apart from her, and Melody inclined her head towards the door. 'After you, Professor Wilmont.' She gestured, indicating he should precede her.

'Ladies first,' he insisted, and the smile he aimed in her direction was one that turned her insides to mush.

She was knocked off guard by the sensation, so mumbled a 'Thank you,' as she went through the door before him.

As they headed towards the operating theatres, Melody pointed out different areas of the hospital, trying to regain her inner composure. It had been quite some time since she'd reacted like this to a man's charming personality, and the outcome of that experience had been one of heartbreak. If she was focusing on playing host, on being professional and imparting information, then her mind couldn't dwell on the unexpected way she was responding to Professor Wilmont.

Once in Theatres, they did a tour of the operating room George would be using when he taught. It had a viewing gallery positioned on a mezzanine floor surrounding the operating table so that students, interns, nursing staff and doctors could easily see what was happening.

'It's also equipped with microphones and miniature cameras. There are two television monitors in the viewing gallery and, as would be expected, we'll be recording the procedures for further study of your techniques.'

'An impressive facility,' George murmured.

'I'm delighted to hear that. I'll pass your comments onto the CEO,' she responded, before they continued with their tour. They headed down yet another long corridor and it was only when George spoke that she realised how close he was to her.

'This is the one characteristic all big hospitals have—long corridors.' His soft, deep tones washed over her and Melody smiled, pleased to find he had a sense of humour.

'And this one has lovely paintings to glance at as people stride by in a rush,' she pointed out.

'True.' There was a wistful note in his tone. 'It's the same in every hospital we've visited. Busy people, rushing here and there and never really stopping to…gaze at the art.' He pointed to a painting of native Australian animals, his pace slowing marginally as he spoke.

'I presume life has been very hectic on your tour?'

'Yes. On the go, non-stop, busy, busy, busy.'

'Have you had any time off during the tour?' she asked as they walked along together.

'We had a month off in June. It was needed by then because we'd all been living in each other's pockets for the past five months. Plus, we get every Saturday off—if we're not flying somewhere, that is. Carmel's very organised.' There was the slightest hint of sadness in his tone and she wondered why. Was he sad that the tour was almost at an end? Would he miss jet-setting around the world, being adored and praised for his innovative surgical techniques?

'How do you cope with the jet-lag?'

'Stay hydrated and sleep on the plane.' George recited the phrase as though he'd said it over and over. 'Actually, the jet-lag hasn't been too bad because we've done small hops between countries, but when we arrived back in Australia three weeks ago we took a week off to acclimatise ourselves to the Aussie weather, especially as we landed in Darwin.'

'Wise decision, and October is still nice and mild compared to summer.'

'I've missed it, though.'

'The Australian summer?' She looked at him as though he was crazy, given that summer temperatures were usually exceedingly hot.

He laughed. 'Yes. The heat, the people, the accent. You have no idea how great it was to hear that Aussie twang at the airport.'

Melody smiled as she pressed the button for the lift. When he laughed like that, when his smile was full, she was astonished to discover her knees weakening at the sound. He really was handsome. When she'd been planning for the visiting orthopaedic surgeon's tour, she hadn't given a lot of thought to what type of man he might be. She'd just expected him to be a surgeon who was intent on explaining his operating techniques and research projects, before moving onto the next hospital to do the same thing. She hadn't expected him to have a sense of humour that matched her own. She also hadn't expected to be so instantly attracted to a married man—something she normally avoided.

Ian had been married. Of course, he hadn't told her that until they'd been dating for three months. She frowned as she thought about the first man to break her heart but when George looked her way, Melody quickly pushed all thoughts of the past from her mind and concentrated on the present.

Professor Wilmont had a lecture to give in twenty minutes and she needed to get him to the venue without mishap. The lift bell dinged and a moment later the doors opened. 'All right, can everyone fit in?' Melody asked as she held the doors open. 'Everyone in?' When she received affirmative murmurs, she allowed the doors to close and pressed the button for the fifth floor. She refused to focus on the way George was standing right behind her, nice and close, the natural warmth from his body causing a wave of tingles to spread over her. She also refused to allow the fresh spicy scent he wore to wind its way about her senses. Why weren't these lifts bigger?

She cleared her throat and forced her mind back into gear. 'The hospital's main lecture facility, which is where you'll be giving most of your lectures, had a complete upgrade last year,' she informed them. 'I've been assured that all the gadgets are in working order but if you find we don't have everything you require, please let me know.'

'Thank you.' George replied, his tone as polite and professional as Melody's, yet she could have sworn she saw a slight smirk touch the corners of his lips. Was she entertaining him? Or had he simply heard similar spiels at different hospitals around the globe? When the lift doors opened, they all exited, again George waiting until Melody had preceded him. She nodded politely before leading the way to the lecture room.

When she pushed open the large double doors, George's team instantly fanned out to check the facilities. One of his assistants headed to the audiovisual desk to connect his computer to the system, another did a sound check. They scuttled back and forth, checking things with each other and ensuring the slides and short snippets of operating techniques were ready to go.

George walked over to the podium, where Carmel gave him several instructions as well as handing him a folder with notes inside. He familiarised himself with where his water glass would be, where to find the laser pointer and how to adjust the lapel microphone.

Melody wandered over to a seat in the front row and sat down, mesmerised by the confidence he exuded—and he wasn't even giving a speech. Lecturing wasn't one of her strong suits so she was always willing to learn. Just by watching him, she knew she could learn a great deal.

Is that the real reason you're watching him? The question crept into the back of her mind before she could stop it. She'd been doing her best to think of him as Professor Wilmont rather than George, as he'd instructed, but as she sat there, gazing at him, she realised she already thought of him as George. He was a very personable man but, then, he'd need to be in order to carry out the duties of the travelling fellowship. She tilted her head to the side, her gaze following his every move. He was classically tall, dark and extremely handsome.

There was no denying to herself that she found George… intriguing, which made him a man to be avoided at all costs. The last man who had 'intrigued' her, Emir, had broken her heart into tiny pieces and discarded her as though she was nothing more than an inconvenient diversion. One broken engagement was more than enough for Melody, so the last thing she should be doing right now was ogling a married man.

Then again, the irrational side of her mind pointed out, there was no harm in looking, right? She closed her eyes to block out the image of George and concentrated on controlling her warring psyche. Professor Wilmont would be gone at the end of the week, finishing the rest of his tour. He'd be gone and she'd be here, still trying to focus on the duties of being acting head of department. Their worlds were miles apart and the only thing they had in common was that they were both orthopaedic surgeons.

Someone sat in the chair next to her, bringing her out of her reverie. Was it time for people to start arriving for

George's first lecture already? She opened her eyes, only to find she was face to face with the man himself. 'Sleeping? I'm not boring you already, am I?' George's deep baritone washed over her.

Melody smiled. 'Not sleeping, just thinking.'

'You were right. This is a great lecture room. One of the better ones.'

'I'm glad.'

'When I visited Bangladesh, I did this same talk in a small annexe next to the hospital. Dirt floors, tin roof, more like a lean-to, and everyone who came huddled around my computer to watch the slides and short recordings I showed.' He nodded. 'It was one of my best talks because I was so relaxed.'

'You're not relaxed today?'

He shrugged one shoulder and checked his tie was securely in place. 'I didn't have to wear a suit there either. Far too hot. How anyone can be completely relaxed whilst wearing a suit, I don't know.'

'You don't like wearing a suit?' There was a hint of incredulity in her words. 'Surely, on this tour, you've had to wear one most days.'

'Yep.'

'Then why do the tour in the first place?'

For the first time since she'd met him she saw a hint of sadness in his eyes but he quickly looked away, checking his watch. 'People should start arriving soon.'

'Yes.' A strange awkwardness seemed to settle over them, although Melody had no idea why. She'd asked what she had thought to be a general question and George's whole demeanour had changed from light-hearted to sad to professional. She wanted to ask why, not to pry but because she was genuinely concerned, but, then, the visiting professor's psyche was none of her business. 'Er…you certainly have a great team,' she stated, taking her lead from him and keeping their conversation to a strictly professional line. 'A well-oiled machine.'

'They certainly are. At first it was all rather strange, having people ordering me about every step of the way, but now, after months of travelling and lecturing, I've learned to trust them. They're all extremely good at their jobs, and if we each do our own thing and avoid getting in each other's way, then things generally run smoothly.'

'I guess that's the name of the game when you're on one of these visiting professorships.'

'Absolutely. Besides, in spending so much time together, we've also become friends.' He gestured to where Carmel was discussing something with Diana, one of the administrative assistants. 'Carmel's amazing. How she keeps all the schedules and travel details and names of people correct, I'll never know.'

'It's definitely a skill.' Melody was equally impressed. 'My PA, Rick, has the same knack. Give me a scalpel over a mound of paperwork any day.' She chuckled. People were starting to arrive and take their seats.

'Making friends with your work colleagues can be an advantage. Of course, when you're a small group, it can sometimes be dangerous.' George sighed as he continued to watch Carmel and Diana.

'Dangerous?' She followed his gaze, picking up on the wistfulness of his tone. Was George involved with Carmel or Diana? Relationships were bound to happen in such a small group that spent so much time together.

'Carmel and Diana.' George shrugged one shoulder. 'They've been on and off again for most of the trip, I can't keep up any more.' As the two women smiled warmly at each other, George nodded. 'Definitely on again at the moment.' Carmel finished talking to Diana, then turned and beckoned to George. 'I'm being summoned.'

'Off to work, Professor,' Melody said with a smile, and as George stood, he returned her smile—a bright, happy smile that made her feel all fluttery and feminine. Why? Why would she feel like that because a handsome man smiled at her?

George listened to what Carmel had to say but his thoughts were still with the delightful Melody Janeway. It wasn't often he met people he instantly connected with, so when it happened it took him by surprise. He glanced once more at Melody, who was now talking with Rick.

'George?' Carmel snapped her fingers at him and he immediately returned his attention to his PA. 'Focus.'

'I'm focused, Carmel.' He chuckled at the way she'd snapped her fingers at him. That usually meant she was in organisational mode. 'I like relaxed, chatty Carmel better than Ms Hospital Corners.'

'Tough.' She handed him the laser pointer then walked over to Melody. George watched as Melody chatted with both PAs before standing and heading to the podium. She moved with grace and ease, smoothing a hand down her skirt before adjusting her papers. She held herself perfectly, her back straight, her shoulders square as she read from the notes, glancing up to look at the assembled crowd. Her voice was clear and her words well modulated. He liked listening to her talk.

Before too long, she was turning to face him, smiling at him, and he realised he hadn't heard a word she'd said. He'd been so captivated by this new acquaintance that he really had drifted off into la-la land. What was wrong with him? It wasn't like him to behave in such a fashion, and especially not when he was standing in front of a large crowd of people—people who were all looking at him expectantly.

He needed to pull on his professionalism, to brush aside any intriguing thoughts he had about Melody Janeway, and do the job he'd been sent to do. He was Professor George Wilmont, orthopaedic surgeon, and widower. He was not a man who experienced an instant attraction towards a colleague, or acted on it.

This time, when he politely shook her hand to thank her for introducing him, he exuded a cool reserve. This time there was no jolt of awareness. This time he was the consummate professional and he was determined to remain so for the rest of his stay in Sydney.

CHAPTER TWO

LUNCH WAS A lavish affair for a 'few' special guests—all fifty of them. Thankfully, as St Aloysius Hospital was situated in the heart of Sydney, there were a plethora of delightful restaurants in the vicinity, and Melody knew Rick had booked several of them for lunches and dinners throughout the week.

When she'd arrived, she'd discovered that she was seated next to George. The scent of his spicy aftershave teased at her senses, making her aware of his nearness. Closing her eyes for a moment, Melody composed herself, needing to remain polite but professional.

She'd never had the greatest luck with men, as her older brothers, David and Ethan, would attest. After her last break-up, one that had fed the hospital gossips for a good six months at least, she'd decided to focus on her career. Two years later, she was now where she wanted to be, but she was also lonely, spending more and more hours at the hospital in order to curtail the emotion.

When would it be her turn to find an honest man? A man who wanted to settle down and start a family? A man who wasn't already married, or who believed in monogamy? *Probably when you become brave enough to date again,* her head answered her heart. She had been shy, not wanting to put herself out there again, hoping that fate would simply bring the right man to her doorstep.

She glanced at George Wilmont, watching as he chatted animatedly with the doctor seated on the other side of him. She liked the way his lips curved into a smile, the way his deep, rich tones could wash over her and ease away her tensions. No man had ever turned her head, made her laugh and captured her interest as quickly as George Wilmont.

Melody forced herself to look away. She needed to rein in her crazy romantic notions and her desperation to find the man who was her soul mate, because George Wilmont was definitely *not* that man. At the moment she should view him as nothing more than a handsome diversion who would leave at the end of the week.

When the time came for George to say a few words, Melody accepted her notes from Rick, who was really earning the title of 'right-hand man', and headed to the podium. After she'd once again introduced George, he'd thanked her but this time when he'd smiled her way, it hadn't been the polite professional mask he'd had in the lecture theatre. No, this time, while she'd been standing at the podium in a room full of her peers, George had decided to hit her with a one hundred percent, full-watt smile.

The pep-talk she'd just given herself vanished from her mind as she allowed herself to be dazzled by him. She might have even gasped at the sight but her mind hadn't been functioning properly, given his enigmatic presence, so she wasn't certain.

What she *was* certain about, however, was the way her body seemed to be tuning itself to George's frequency without her permission. In fact, once he'd given his short talk and returned to sit beside her, his spicy cologne once more started to wind its way around her, causing a devastating effect on her equilibrium. She didn't want to be so aware of him, yet she was.

She focused on the conversation taking place about the latest medical breakthrough, listening intently to George's opinion on the subject. During their entrée and main course, George answered many questions. It was a rare opportunity to have access to someone who was travelling the world, hearing and seeing at first-hand new innovations in the ever-changing orthopaedic world, and her colleagues were making the most of it.

Just as their desserts were being brought around, George stood and removed his suit jacket. Melody found her gaze drawn to his movements and she watched from beneath her lashes, mesmerised by the way his triceps flexed beneath the material of his shirt. It almost made her hyperventilate. She took a sip from her water glass, breathing in as she swallowed.

Melody spluttered and started to cough. George patted her on the back and everyone at their table stopped talking and watched her.

'You all right, Melody?' George asked as he sat down again.

His concern was touching and she looked at him with an embarrassed grin. She coughed again and nodded. 'I'm…' another cough '…fine.' She didn't sound fine, even to her own ears, as the word had come out like a tiny squeak. Melody cleared her throat. 'Fine,' she reiterated more strongly. Everyone resumed their conversations and she'd half expected George to continue talking to Carmel. Instead, he leaned over and refilled her water glass.

'Try it again.' He held the glass out to her and she took it, their fingertips touching—just for an instant. It was enough to spread a deep warmth throughout her body, causing her to gasp quietly. She was so aware of him it was ridiculous. Why couldn't she control these sensations?

Her smile faded but she did as he suggested, conscious of the way he watched her actions. Their gazes held and Melody found herself powerless to look away. She rested the glass on her lower lip. As she tilted the liquid towards her mouth, she exhaled slowly, her breath steaming up the glass. She sipped and swallowed, replacing the glass on the table before her trembling fingers dropped it.

'There,' he whispered, but didn't smile. 'All better.' His gorgeous brown eyes were intense. Melody felt momentarily hypnotised. Within an instant George had somehow made her feel…desirable.

'George will know.' Carmel's voice intruded into the little bubble that surrounded them.

George tried desperately to listen to what Carmel was asking, all the while trying to figure out what had just happened with Melody Janeway. He'd been mesmerised by her again. Was it the way her lips had trembled ever so slightly as she'd rested the glass on her lip? Or the way they'd parted to allow the liquid to pass between them. He swallowed convulsively and pushed thoughts of her from his mind, even though he seemed conscious of her every move.

Carmel was still talking and although George could see her lips moving, he was having great difficulty in concentrating. Thankfully, the last few words sank in and he was able to answer the question in an authoritative and controlled manner.

Melody rose to her feet and quietly excused herself. George glanced at her, noticing the way she smoothed her skirt down over her thighs. It wasn't the first time she'd done it and he wondered if it meant she was nervous. Not that he was objecting to the action, for each time she did it, it drew attention to her gorgeous legs.

Why was she nervous? Had she felt that unmistakable pull of attraction between them? Or was she always this jittery? He wouldn't know. He didn't know the woman and yet the sensations he felt when around her had occurred several times during their very short acquaintance. It was like nothing he'd experienced before but he'd assumed the sensations were solely on his side. *Did* she feel it? The question kept reverberating around at the back of his mind as he tried to concentrate on the discussion at their table.

A mouth-watering chocolate dessert was placed before him but he pushed it away, not interested. He'd had enough of food—for the moment.

'Are you all right?' Carmel asked quietly, leaning closer to him to ensure her words didn't carry to the other people around them.

'Fine. Why?'

'Because you can't seem to stop staring at our hostess for this week.'

George was stunned at his friend's words. 'What? I wasn't staring at her,' he whispered vehemently.

'It's OK, George. It just means you're normal and Melody is a very attractive woman, but not my type. Definitely more your type.'

'I don't have a type. I'm in mourning.'

'You can't stay in mourning for ever, George. You and I both know that's not the life Veronique would have wanted for you. Besides,' Carmel continued quickly before he could say anything, 'it's not every day a woman really captures your attention. Melody's the first I've noticed you taking an interest in throughout the entire tour.'

'That doesn't mean to say I'm going to act on it.'

'Aha. You *do* like her. I knew it.'

'Shh.' George glanced around them but no one seemed to be paying them much attention. They would just think that he and Carmel were discussing aspects of the schedule. 'Whether I like her or not is irrelevant. We have a hectic schedule to get through and then we'll be gone at the end of the week.'

'We're off to Perth.'

'Perth, Adelaide or anywhere in between, I don't care. The point is that I have a life waiting for me in Melbourne.'

'What life?'

'I have a house. A job.'

'Things you couldn't wait to leave behind when the fellowship began,' she reminded him.

George pursed his lips, knowing she had a point. When the tour had started, he couldn't wait to leave Melbourne, to leave the grief of his life without Veronique behind. Although he was looking forward to a less hectic pace of life, he wasn't sure Melbourne would hold the same charms for him as it had before. He knew that with everything he'd seen and experienced on this tour, he was a very different man from the one who had left, eager to escape his grief.

Carmel glanced momentarily down at her phone, which had buzzed with a message. 'It's the little things in life that mean the most,' Carmel stated a moment later, a soft smile on her lips.

'Message from Diana?' he asked, gesturing to her phone.

Carmel's smile increased. 'Yes.'

'You've managed to sort things out, then?'

'Yes. Diana was jealous of that redhead we met in Darwin but I've assured her there was nothing going on between us. We just had to work closely together, just like this week I'm working closely with Rick and Melody.'

'I'm glad you're back together. It's more harmonious for the rest of us,' George couldn't help but tease. He was glad Carmel was the one who had come on the tour with him. The fact that she'd been the director for other travelling fellowships and had been helping Veronique to organise this one when tragedy had struck—well—George was glad it was Carmel who had come, especially as she and Veronique had been good friends. Carmel had known his wife, had known how happy the two of them had been together, so to hear her now say that it was OK not to deny his instant connection with Melody Janeway was almost a relief.

Carmel chuckled at his words, then noticed Melody walking back towards their table. 'Finding harmony in your life is a good thing, George.'

George followed Carmel's gaze, his whole being mesmerised by the way Melody walked. She was so graceful, like a dancer, hovering momentarily to talk to someone before continuing her way back to him. 'You haven't been captivated by anyone since Veronique, which definitely means there's something about Melody that has caught your attention.'

Carmel's words floated over him in the background as George noticed that the small auburn curl that had escaped the bonds of the clip was now securely back in place. He wondered if her hair colour was natural. Either way, he knew it suited her and made the green of her eyes seem more intense.

He forced himself to look away as she sat back down, trying his best not to be affected by the allure of the floral scent she wore. He was intrigued by her, interested to get to know her better and the knowledge troubled him. Carmel had been right when she'd said that no other woman had captivated him, not the way Melody Janeway had. What was it about his new colleague that was causing him to behave in such a way?

'Feeling better?' he asked, and she smiled politely in his direction, the smile causing his gut to tighten with a need he'd thought repressed.

'Yes, thank you. It was—um—silly of me to choke on the water like that. Then again,' she said with a small chuckle, 'I'm usually the person who drops their knife on the floor and or spills food on their shirt.'

With that, George's gaze instantly dropped to her shirt to check if she'd done just that. When he realised he was staring at her breasts, he instantly focused his gaze back on her lovely green eyes. 'You're in the clear today.'

'So far,' she remarked jestingly, and he returned her smile.

'Were you clumsy as a child?'

Melody pondered his words for a moment. 'Not clumsy exactly…or at least not that I can recall. I'm sure if you asked my brothers, they'd have a different story.'

'Older brothers?' George was delighted she was talking to him about her personal life. He wanted to know about her, he wanted to know what made her laugh, what thrilled her, what made her sad. Perhaps Carmel was right and he should just accept the little moments of happiness he could experience.

'Yes, but thankfully as we've grown older, they don't treat me like I'm completely useless. Now we're all good friends. How about you?' Melody couldn't stop herself from wanting to know more about him, about things that weren't contained in the professional dossier she'd been sent months ago. 'Any siblings?'

He nodded. 'I have younger twin sisters who still love to stick their noses into my life.'

'My brothers aren't twins, there's eighteen months between them, but as I'm four years younger, the two of them did a lot of things together and I always felt like left out.'

'I'm like that with my sisters. They've always had each other.'

'There you go, then. We're both the odd ones out in our families.' She picked up her glass and held it out to him. He quickly clinked his against hers, and they both sipped. Their gazes held again and she felt her smile begin to fade. That underlying tug of attraction was starting to wind its way around them and she desperately fought for something to say that would break the moment. 'You haven't touched your dessert. Don't you have a sweet tooth?'

'Not really. I used to before I started this tour but I've had so many working dinners and lunches—even breakfasts—that my sweet tooth has definitely disappeared.'

'That's a lot of food.'

'Absolutely.' He smiled. 'But it gives me the opportunity to speak to more people, to get the word out about new advances, new techniques, and that's one of the main aims of visiting professorships.'

'Excuse me, Melody,' Rick interrupted. 'I've just had a call from Mr Okanadu's office.'

'Problem?'

'One of his private patients is having complications.'

'He's gone to Theatre,' Melody stated, and automatically checked her watch. Rick nodded.

'Something wrong?' Carmel asked, her radar ears picking up the conversation.

'Mr Okanadu, the surgeon who was scheduled to assist George in Theatre this afternoon, has called through with an emergency.'

Carmel thought calmly for a moment, then indicated to Melody. 'I'm sure you wouldn't mind stepping into the breach, Melody.'

'Me?' Melody looked from George to Carmel to Rick, then back to Carmel. 'Surely there's someone—'

'You're a qualified orthopaedic surgeon,' Carmel stated. 'And I'm fairly sure, being the thorough professional that you are, you've already read the information packet sent to all host hospitals regarding the techniques George will be teaching.'

'She has,' Rick chimed in. 'And she chose the patient. She was putting Mr Barnes's mind at ease this morning before ward round, telling him he'll have the best surgeon in the world performing the operation.'

'Best surgeon, eh?' George drawled, a glorious smile lighting his face, his brown eyes twinkling with delight.

The effect was mind-numbing and Melody wasn't at all sure she'd be able to keep herself under control while standing opposite him in Theatre. At the moment, she was glad she was still sitting down as she wasn't sure her legs would have continued supporting her. What was it about his smile that seemed to make her body melt and her mind go blank?

'So it's settled,' Carmel stated, then rushed off to tell the rest of the team.

'Where is she going?' Melody asked.

'To make the necessary changes. Every day, an extensive diary is kept about who operated on whom and where and when and everything else. The slides for the presentation will need to be changed, your name inserted instead of Dr Okanadu's…' He trailed off and shrugged. 'That sort of thing.'

'Would you mind quickly going over the procedure again with me? Just talk me through the highlights,' she stated. Although she had read up on the procedure, now that she'd been forced into this, she wanted to do an excellent job.

Before George could answer, someone came over from another table and commandeered his attention, leaving Melody sitting there, trying her best to remember what she'd read.

'You OK, boss?' Rick asked, pulling up a chair beside her.

'No.'

'Oh? What's the problem?'

'I don't want to assist.'

'You'd rather be up in the gallery, squashed in all hot and bothered, telling people to shush so you could hear what was being said?' He paused. 'Now you get to be a part of the action, Melody. It's an honour and a privilege and you'll have the best view in the house.'

'I guess when you put it that way…' The one thing she wasn't looking forward to were the small sensual bursts of tension she seemed to experience whenever George was near. She would have to work extra-hard on her self-control and professionalism in Theatre.

Accepting her fate, Melody reached for her water glass again and drank the contents. That would be her last drink until she came out of Theatre. At least she hadn't choked on this drink. Surely that was a good sign that she wouldn't make a fool of herself. Right?

CHAPTER THREE

'SUCTION,' GEORGE ORDERED, and Melody complied. They'd been in Theatre for almost four hours now and George looked as fresh as when he'd first walked in. At first Melody had been very conscious of the packed viewing gallery but once the operation had begun, she'd pushed it to the back of her mind. She had a job to do and they owed it to their patient to do just that.

They still had an hour to go on the pelvic reconstruction. George's research in this field had led him to invent a device that made certain aspects of the surgery more manageable. He'd been extensively published in several of the world's leading orthopaedic journals, hence why he'd been chosen for this visiting professorship. And here she was—operating alongside him. She couldn't quite take it in.

'Now we'll start reducing the posterior aspect of the fracture. I'll be fixing one eight-hole, three-and-a-half-millimetre reconstruction plate, securing it in place with two screws at either end.' George spoke in his normal tone, knowing his words would be picked up on the microphone that was situated within the theatre.

When the viewing gallery had been built, the actual operating room had undergone a transformation as well. Small cameras had been installed, enabling everyone to see the procedure being performed. Apart from general teaching, this was the first time the theatre had been used for a visiting specialist.

'I'll need an inter-fragmentary screw as well to keep that acetabular margin firmly in place,' George said once the reconstruction plate had been positioned.

'Swab.' A few moments later, George glanced at Melody and she read the satisfaction in his gaze. The look made her feel as though they were sharing a special secret. 'I'm happy with that,' he stated. 'Check X-ray, please.' While they waited for the radiographer to take the X-ray, George looked up at the viewing gallery and explained some of the finer points of the surgery he'd just performed.

Melody allowed herself a brief glance up, only to see several heads in the gallery bowed as students, interns and registrars alike furiously took notes. Thanks to the cameras, though, it meant a permanent record would be kept of this procedure so anyone who had missed it could view it online through the hospital's link.

Melody had never been so relieved to walk out of theatre and into the changing rooms, leaving George to finish answering questions and the theatre staff to clean up. Operating with him had been a wonderful experience, but during the first few minutes of the procedure she'd been so acutely aware of him that her heart had been beating a wild tattoo against her ribs. Forcing her professionalism to the fore, Melody had pretended he was just like anyone else she'd operated with.

Although she hadn't been the centre of attention, Melody had still felt as though she were trapped like a mouse in a cage. All those people, watching everything they did. 'Relax,' she told herself as she had a quick shower. 'It's over.' Everything had gone fine. There had been no complications, no awkward moments. George had been very explicit in what he'd wanted each member of staff to do and Melody realised he was used to operating with strangers.

As she dried herself and headed to her locker, she knew

there was no way she'd ever be able to cope with the pressures of a visiting professorship. She was a good surgeon and that was all she wanted. The opportunity to do further research into micro-surgical techniques of the hand and fingers was definitely enough to keep her occupied for quite some time.

She was just tucking in her shirt when two of the nurses who had been in Theatre with them came in.

'Hot-diggity,' Hilary said, fanning her face. 'He is one gorgeous man. Pity he's married.' Hilary giggled. 'Not that that would stop me.' She covered her mouth. 'Oops. Naughty me.'

'I thought he was a widower.' Evelyn angled her head to the side. 'That's what one of his assistants told me.' Evelyn looked at Melody. 'Have you heard anything, Melody?'

'About what?' Melody started to brush her curls. She hated gossip. When she'd been engaged to Emir, there had been a lot of gossip going on about her. Not only had Emir been cheating on her with several women, one of them had fallen pregnant. If it hadn't been for Evelyn, who had come and told Melody the truth about Emir's infidelities, she would have still been living in cloud cuckoo land.

Before she'd confronted her fiancé, a distraught Melody had asked her brother, Ethan, to make some discreet enquiries. When Ethan had confirmed it, Melody had called off the engagement. Then Emir had told her a German doctor was carrying his child and that the two of them were moving to Germany to raise their family.

That had hurt more than anything. Prior to their engagement, Emir had been adamant that he never wanted to have children. Melody had taken months to come to terms with the fact that she'd never be a mother if she married Emir and eventually she'd accepted that. Then to have him turn around and say he was more than willing to be a father to another woman's child had made Melody realise that Emir simply hadn't wanted to have children with *her*.

He hadn't wanted *her*. He hadn't respected *her*. He hadn't truly loved *her*.

'About Professor Wilmont!' Hilary exclaimed, bringing Melody's thoughts back to the present. 'Honestly, Melody, you should get out from behind that desk or operating table or whatever it is you hide behind more often because that man is *so* hot.'

Melody clipped her unruly auburn hair back in its usual style. 'He's a great surgeon. That's what I know about him,' she replied. There was no way she was going to tell them that he set her blood pumping, made her knees go weak and took her breath away all with one smouldering, sexy look. She closed her locker. 'Are you both coming to the dinner tonight?'

'I have another shift,' Evelyn said.

'I couldn't afford it.' Hilary actually pouted. 'And lucky you—you get to sit next to him.'

'Enjoy it,' Evelyn offered with a genuine smile before Melody walked out of the room and headed back to her office. She needed to check her in-tray and make sure everything was up to date. Rick was absent from his desk, so she headed directly into her office and almost jumped in fright when she saw George seated comfortably next to her desk.

'George! I thought you'd gone.' And how had he changed so quickly? Her stomach lurched in delight at the sight of him, and her knees started to weaken. She told herself off for behaving like a ninny and forced her legs to work, walking over to her desk before quickly sitting.

'I wanted to thank you personally for assisting me at such short notice.'

Her smile was instant. 'It should be me who's thanking you for the opportunity. Or should I thank Mr Okanadu's emergency?'

George chuckled and the sound washed over her, warming her even further. 'Either way, it was great to be able to work with you.'

'You made everything easy for me—and the rest of the staff,' she added. She looked at him for a second, tilting her head to the side. 'Are you always so…direct in Theatre or is it just because you have an audience?'

He nodded. 'It's the audience. I've become accustomed to having people watch me.'

'Well, you're certainly very good at what you do.' She idly shifted some paper around before placing her hands palms down on the desk in an effort to control her wayward emotions. How was it that just his close presence was enough to turn her into a jittery, hormonal mess? The intercom buzzed and she was glad of something to do. She pressed the button. 'Yes, Rick?'

'I'm going now, Melody.'

'All right. See you tonight, Rick.'

'Yeah, but only if I can tie that bow-tie thing straight. Who made it a formal dinner, eh?'

'We can blame Carmel,' George called loudly, and Rick chuckled before saying goodbye. 'He's good,' George said. 'How long has he been working with you?'

'No.' Melody shook her head. 'The question you should be asking is how long have I been working with him? He's been the PA to the head of orthopaedics for the past three years. I only started six months ago.'

'How old is he? He looks about seventeen.'

'Shh.' Melody giggled. 'Don't tell him that. He's still trying to fight his cute baby face looks. He's twenty-four and an excellent PA.' Melody pulled her bag out of a drawer before locking her desk. 'When the head of department was taken ill at the beginning of this year, it was Rick who helped me find my feet. Without him, I'd have gone down the gurgler ages ago.'

'So you're not into hospital politics? Administration?'

'Not really.' Melody stood and motioned to the door. 'We'd better make a move or we'll end up being late for dinner.'

'Sure.' George followed her out of her office and waited while she locked it. Melody turned and bumped into him. She hadn't realised he'd been standing so close.

'Sorry,' she mumbled, and quickly took a step to the side. She glanced down at the floor, trying desperately to control the mass of tingles that were now raging rampantly throughout her body. Melody kept her head down as she moved a few steps away before raising her head to look at him. One of her curls managed to escape from its bonds and swung down beside her cheek.

To her astonishment, George reached out a hand towards her, as though he intended to tuck her hair behind her ear. Melody held her breath, her gaze darting erratically from his hand to his face and back to his hand again. Then George swallowed and dropped his hand back to his side, shoving it into his pocket. He clenched his jaw and took a step back, then glanced at her briefly before looking away, the moment slipping by.

'Ah—are you—? I mean—do you—um…?' She stopped and forced herself to take a steadying breath. 'How are you getting back to the hotel? Do you need a lift?'

George nodded, a slow smile forming on his lips. 'That would be great. Thanks.'

'Car park is this way.' Without waiting for further communication from him, Melody headed off down the corridor and turned right at the end. She opened a door and started heading down the stairs. She was acutely aware of George following her and it wasn't until they'd gone down three flights of stairs that she pushed open the door that led to the street.

'I'm parked over here,' she told him as they walked side by side.

'So, the previous head of orthopaedics? You said he was taken ill?'

'Yes, in February. He was working out this year and had planned to retire at the end of it. Now he's retired early.'

'So he's not coming back?'

'No. He's officially resigned from the hospital.'

'Which leaves you in charge?'

'They have to advertise the position. I'm only Acting Head until the end of this year,' she told him as she stopped by her white Jaguar Mark II. She unlocked the door. 'So when you finish your tour, do you want a job?' She chuckled, but even the thought of working closely with George day in, day out filled her with a mass of tingles. She pushed the idea aside.

'*This* is your car?' George frowned in disbelief.

'Yep.' Melody climbed in and reached over to unlock the passenger door. 'One thing about old cars, they don't usually come with the mod-cons like central locking,' she said as George slid onto the comfortable leather seat.

'Wow.'

'I know, right? Such an awesome car. I love it.' She put her seat belt on. 'It was a present from my brothers when I passed my final orthopaedic exams. David's a mechanic,' she added by way of explanation. 'Both he and Ethan like restoring old cars.'

'Are they both mechanics?'

She chuckled as she put the key into the ignition before starting the engine. 'Ethan likes to think he is but he's more a mechanic of people—also known as a general surgeon.'

'Huh. Does he work at St Aloysius as well? I'd like to meet him.'

'He used to.' Melody chatted as she began to exit the car park. 'Ethan used to be Head of General Surgery but earlier this year he had a mild heart attack. He's OK now,' she added, then grinned. 'More than OK, actually, as he recently got married.' Melody sighed romantically. 'It was a wonderful wedding in the lovely wine district, just inland of Sydney.'

'Around Whitecorn?' he asked, and she was surprised.

'Yes. Pridham and Whitecorn hospitals. That's where he now works as a general surgeon.'

'I have friends there. Donna and Philip Spadina. Donna tutored me through medical school.'

'What? Ethan and CJ's wedding was *at* Donna and Philip's small vineyard.'

'Ah… I love being back in Australia,' he sighed. 'Everyone knows someone who knows someone else. Nice and close.'

She chuckled. 'Have you been homesick for Australia?'

'Just a bit.'

'Has it been difficult, jet-setting around the world, showing off your brilliance?' Melody couldn't resist teasing lightly. Oh, my gosh, she thought. I'm flirting with him! George laughed and the sound washed over her with joy. She'd made him laugh. Evelyn's words floated in the back of her mind, stating that she thought George was a widower. Was it true?

'The beginning was difficult, getting into the swing of things, but then it evened out. Now I think this part of the tour is the most…tedious.' He shifted in his chair, turning to face her slightly. 'I don't mean to imply that I don't like being here at St Aloysius—or any other hospital, for that matter.'

'It's OK, George. I understood what you meant. It's not the work, it's the day-to-day grind, especially when the end is so close.'

'Thank you.' He shook his head. 'You get it. Carmel's fretting because she doesn't want it to end.'

'Perhaps she doesn't know what she's going to be doing when this is over.'

'That would bring uncertainty,' he mused, as though he hadn't considered it.

'What about you? What happens after you've written up all your reports and caught up with your friends?'

George sighed. 'I'll go back to my job at Melbourne General, I guess.'

'You guess?'

He chuckled. 'I don't know what I'm going to feel like doing. It's as though my life's in limbo but it's where I need to start in order to figure out what to do next.' George slowly shook his head, then changed the subject, turning the spotlight on her. 'And what about you? Are you going to apply for the job you're doing now?'

Melody tried to focus her thoughts. 'Probably not.'

'You *really* don't like the administration?'

'Not particularly. How about you?'

'It doesn't bother me. Especially after this year.'

'I guess you don't get much time to relax.'

'Not really. Depending on where we are or what we're doing, I sometimes get a bit of free time.' George shrugged, as though he didn't really care one way or the other.

Melody didn't envy him at all. For a moment she wasn't sure what to say and the silence began to stretch. *Say something*, she told herself. Anything to break the awkwardness that was enveloping both of them. 'So I guess the VOS definitely cuts into your family time.'

He glanced at her and frowned. Oops. Had she overstepped the mark?

She was just about to apologise for her statement when he said, 'It's not too bad. I managed to see one of my sisters when I was in New Zealand so that was a bonus.'

It was Melody's turn to frown as she pulled into the entrance of the hotel. The fact that he hadn't mentioned his wife made her wonder if Evelyn's assumption was correct. George glanced her way and saw the frown.

'Something wrong?' he asked.

Melody instantly smiled. 'Everything's fine.' She wanted to blurt out her question, to ask him about his wife, to know one way or the other whether the feelings she was having for him should be quashed or—or what? Was she planning on throwing herself at the handsome surgeon if he turned out to be single? Or was she going to be professional and remain detached? Still, the question seemed to be going round and round in her head like a broken record. Did George have a wife waiting for him in Melbourne or was she—? Melody shook her head and sighed. 'I guess I'll see you a bit later at the dinner.'

'As the dinner is in my honour, you can count on it.' He gave a playful wink as he climbed from the car and shut the door.

Melody drove to her apartment, even more confused than before. Why had he winked? That wink had caused a new wave of tingles to flood her body, had made her heart beat faster and encouraged her to hope that he was, indeed, not married. She wasn't the type of girl to go after a married man, not after Ian. She wasn't the type of girl to suffer from instant infatuation, or at least that's what she'd believed this morning.

Now, after meeting George Wilmont and spending so much time with him today, she knew that if the right man came along, she was definitely prone to instant attraction because that's exactly what she felt for George!

CHAPTER FOUR

GEORGE SCANNED THE crowded outer room that was starting to fill up. When he'd first started on the VOS tour, he'd been astounded at the number of dinners he needed to attend. Now, though, he was an expert at them. At least in his medical lecturing he'd been able to write new lectures, sharing information he'd garnered throughout the tour.

His gaze scanned the room as people started making their way through to the ballroom. He checked his watch. Five minutes over time already. Carmel would become agitated soon. Where was Melody? They couldn't start without her. She was the MC.

He looked around again and realised he'd been unconsciously searching for her the entire time. Someone came up, introduced themselves and shook hands with him. George listened to the questions being asked of him and gave the usual replies, all the while allowing his gaze to flick to the door every few seconds.

'Excuse me.' Carmel politely interrupted his conversation, drawing him to one side. 'It's time to begin.'

'Melody's not here yet,' George pointed out.

'If we wait any longer, we'll be getting to bed after midnight.'

'We'll be getting to bed after midnight anyway.' He smiled wryly at his friend, his eyes pleading. 'We can wait for her, right?'

'Ah…so you *do* like her.' Carmel's tone changed to one of delight. 'I knew it.'

'She's nice. Everyone likes her,' George felt compelled to point out.

'It's OK to like someone, George.' Carmel's words were soft and encouraging. 'You're not meant to spend the rest of your life alone, you know.'

George shrugged a shoulder at his friend's words because he wasn't sure how to respond. He wasn't used to having these sorts of feelings, especially when he carried the memory of his wife with him wherever he went.

Carmel glanced at her phone to check the time. 'We can give her another five minutes and I'm only acquiescing this once because it's great to see you taking a chance to move forward.'

'But I'm not.'

'Lie to me, George, but don't lie to yourself.' She fixed him with a firm stare before heading off.

George exhaled harshly and ran a finger around the collar of his shirt. The room was becoming too stuffy and he sneaked out the door, heading towards the lobby. Was Carmel right? Was he lying to himself? It was true that ever since meeting Melody Janeway that morning, he'd had a difficult time removing her from his thoughts. She was beautiful, intelligent and funny. What a lethal combination!

He checked his watch again. Ten minutes late. Was she lost? Was she at the wrong hotel? Why was she late? Veronique had been three hours late and he'd been telling himself back then not to worry. Yet all the time she'd been— He stopped his train of thought. This was no time to be thinking about Veronique.

As soon as he saw Rick enter the hotel, he almost pounced on him. 'Where's Melody?'

'She's not here yet?' Rick asked in surprise, immediately pulling out his phone.

'No.'

'It's gone straight to voice mail. She's probably at the hospital. I'll ring the ward.'

'Thanks.' George started to relax. At least Melody hadn't been involved in an accident.

'She's just left?' Rick said into the receiver. 'Good. Thanks.' He disconnected the call. 'She left the hospital five minutes ago so she shouldn't be long now. She's a great doctor.' Rick grinned, then shook his head mockingly. 'Pathetic head of department but a great doctor.'

'I guess that's what's important.' George smiled, feeling more at ease. 'Why don't you go and tell Carmel what's happening?' he suggested. 'I'll wait here for Melody.'

'You just don't want to face Carmel,' Rick stated with a knowing nod, and George laughed.

'Caught me out.' As he watched Rick go, he knew that wasn't the reason he didn't want to go in. He wanted to see Melody with his own eyes. To make sure she was OK. There were still other people trickling in so she wasn't all *that* late, even though his aide would disagree. George walked over to the wall and looked unseeingly at a painting. Why? Why was he so anxious to see Melody?

On the drive from the hospital to the hotel, he'd been happy in her company, chatting and getting to know her. With the schedule he'd maintained throughout the tour, he'd rarely had the opportunity to get to know the people he'd worked alongside. Every week it was somewhere new, every week it was giving the same information to a different group of faces. He'd met some lovely people, some overly academic professionals, and some people with no sense of humour whatsoever.

Yet from the moment he'd shaken hands with Melody Janeway, experiencing that instant jolt of awareness, he'd been captivated by her. Her twinkling green eyes, her unruly auburn hair with the odd curl that didn't seem to want to do as it was told. He liked her laugh, he liked the sound of her voice and he liked her intelligence. Never in his life had been so instantly drawn to someone. Was it wrong to want to know her better, or was it foolish not to? As Carmel had said, he wasn't meant to live the rest of his life alone.

'George?'

At the sound of her voice, he spun on his heel and gazed at her. There it was again, that instant jolt of awareness.

'What are you doing out here? I thought you were supposed to have started by now.'

George felt as though he'd just been slugged in the solar plexus. She looked…stunning. Wearing an off-the-shoulder, black beaded dress that shimmered when she walked, Melody was a vision of loveliness. The dress was expertly cut, falling to mid-calf, and moulded superbly to her shape. Her auburn tresses had been wound on top of her head with a few loose tendrils springing down. She wore a necklace with a small square-cut diamond pendant and matching diamond studs in her ears.

'I wanted to wait for you.' His tone was thick with desire. 'I'm glad I did. You look…breath-taking.'

His words were sincere and the way he was looking at her made her feel light-headed. George really thought she was breath-taking? She took a small step closer, her gaze never leaving his. 'Thank you, George. That's a lovely thing to say.'

'And I mean it.'

She smiled brightly, still trying to come to terms with how incredible he looked in his black tuxedo, white shirt and bow-tie. When she'd walked in and seen him, her knees had almost given way and as she was wearing three-inch heels, the result would have been disastrous. Thankfully, she'd been able to hold onto a vestige of control.

George cleared his throat and pasted on a polite smile, crooking his elbow towards her. 'Shall we?'

They headed towards the ballroom and as they headed towards the top table, several people stopped George to ask questions or shake his hand. Melody walked ahead of him and George realised her dress had a split at the back, revealing a generous amount of her legs. Her shapely calves, the indentations of the backs of her knees and a brief glimpse of her thighs.

He swallowed and forced himself to look away, concentrating on the carpet, but once he reached the table, he couldn't help but sneak one last glance at her sexy legs. A few minutes later Melody was at the podium, apologising for the delay as she'd been called to the ward. She spoke so naturally, so confidently and looked so exquisite that afterwards he couldn't remember a word she'd actually said.

Once she'd finished her introduction, George stood and thanked her, pulling his professionalism from thin air so he could concentrate on what he needed to say, rather than on the woman whose floral scent was winding its way around him, creating havoc with his senses.

As he spoke, commanding the attention of the two hundred or so people gathered tonight, Melody began to relax, enjoying listening to his deep, melodious voice. She admired the way he threw in little anecdotes, working his way through his speech without the prompting of notes.

'You didn't do too badly,' Rick later commented, as he crouched by her chair.

'I could say the same thing for your bow-tie. How long did it take you to do that?'

'Ages. I only arrived a few minutes before you and I didn't even have the excuse of having stopping by the hospital.'

Melody raised her eyebrows. 'Checking up on me?' She took a sip from her water glass.

'George was concerned,' Rick told her with a shrug, and pointed to her glass. 'Not drinking tonight?'

She shook her head. 'The patient I saw in the ward may need surgery later.'

'Oh, yeah, you doctors have *all* the fun.' He glanced over to where one particular nurse had caught his attention. 'Er—I'll catch up with you later.' He straightened his bow-tie. 'There are a few nurses I want to impress while I'm dressed like this.'

Melody chuckled as he headed off but his words stayed with her. George had been concerned about her? She sneaked a glance at him as he spoke to someone. Had he really been worried about her, or the dinner starting on time?

Melody's head was starting to spin. She needed some space. She picked up her clutch purse and stood.

George watched Melody walk away from the table, his gaze drawn to the sway of her hips and her gorgeous legs. Why was she so captivating? He forced himself to look away, returning his attention to Carmel, only to realise his aide was watching Melody as well.

In fact, all the men at the table were watching her. 'Wow!' one of them remarked. 'Melody looks—'

'Like a woman,' one of the other men finished, and they all laughed.

George felt his hackles begin to rise. 'Problem?'

'This is the first time Melody's worn a dress to an official departmental function,' someone told him. 'So it's the first opportunity we've had to see her in anything other than business clothes.'

'She sure looks different. If being head of department means Melody dresses like that, she has my support for the job.'

'She's also a colleague of yours.' George's tone was clipped, disgusted by their chauvinism. 'An intellectual woman who is a brilliant surgeon. Please provide her with the respect she deserves.' He knew his tone sounded pompous and arrogant but he didn't care. Women had to work twice as hard as men in this world and Melody had done just that. What she needed was to be respected for that, not for what she chose to wear. 'You were saying, Carmel?' George turned his attention to his aide.

He still found it hard to concentrate on what Carmel was saying, his thoughts caught up with Melody and the fact that she wasn't beside him. He was astonished how much he felt her absence, given that when he'd woken up this morning he hadn't even met her! When she returned, he immediately stood and held the chair for her as she sat.

'Thank you.' She smiled at him and again he felt his gut tighten. Clearing his throat, he included her in the conversation with Carmel, valuing her opinion. Ten minutes later, Melody's phone rang.

'Excuse me.' She fished it from her purse. George was aware of her quiet voice as she spoke and moments later she ended the call. 'It looks as though I'll have to pass on coffee,' she told everyone at the table.

'Emergency?' George asked.

'Yes.' At the interested glances she received, she elaborated. 'Fractured olecranon, radius and ulna. My registrar says the patient is showing signs of compartment syndrome.'

'Can't your registrar deal with it?' Carmel asked hopefully. 'You are the MC, after all.'

'Sorry, but it's a private patient,' Melody explained as she picked up her bag.

'I think she's fulfilled her MC duties for the night,' George told his aide.

When she stood, all the men rose to their feet. 'Oh, please, sit down,' she said with a smile, before turning to George. 'Sorry to run out on your welcome dinner but these things can't be helped.'

George remained standing. 'No need to apologise. Besides, we're almost done.' They shook hands and again Melody felt that warm buzz of excitement spread up her arm. She nodded politely before dropping his hand and walking away from the table. She was stopped a few times on her way out but as the room was filled with people linked to the medical profession, they all understood when she said she had an emergency.

She took the lift down to the ground floor, and while waiting for the valet to collect her car she fought for self control. In less than twenty-four hours she'd met a man who affected her like no one else ever had, and she was having difficulty getting him out of her mind. She drove carefully to the hospital, heading straight for the emergency theatres. She changed into theatre clothes and went in search of her registrar.

'Nice hairdo,' Andy, her registrar, teased, and she laughed.

'How's Mr Potter?'

'Coping well. I've explained what's happening to him and he's signed the consent form. The instruments and theatre are ready. We're just waiting on the all-clear from the anaesthetist.'

'Excellent.' Melody went to see her patient and have a word with the anaesthetist before checking the notes Andy had taken during the evening. When everything was organised, they started to scrub.

Once in Theatre, Melody had her mind in gear and off George Wilmont. She focused her attention on Mr Potter's arm, which he'd injured while playing tennis.

Both she and Andy concentrated on what they were doing but, as always, enjoyed a bit of conversation while performing their duties. 'Glad the VOS is finally under way?' Andy asked.

'Most definitely. One day down, four more to go.' Andy had known she hadn't wanted to act as host for the VOS and had tolerated her mounting apprehensiveness with a cool, calm and collected attitude.

'I take it the dinner went well.'

'Yes.' Melody frowned.

'The VOS seems like a nice guy.'

'Did you manage to get to the viewing gallery this afternoon?'

'I came in late. Couldn't see much. You, on the other hand, certainly had a bird's eye view. How did that happen?'

Melody chuckled and told him about Mr Okanadu's cancellation while she inserted a drain into Mr Potter's arm, which would hopefully ensure against further recurrence of compartment syndrome.

'What was it like? I mean, operating with one of the greats?'

She heard the door to her theatre open but thought nothing of it. 'What was it like? It was scary, that's what it was like.' Melody paused for a moment. 'Not scary assisting George, that part was fine, but having all those people watching? No, thank you.'

'George, eh?' Andy teased. 'On a first-name basis already?'

'What do you expect me to call him? Professor? His Excellency? Brilliant Surgeon?'

The sexiest man alive? She kept that last one to herself but smiled beneath her mask. She heard someone slowly walk around the table and come to stand behind Andy.

Melody frowned and raised her gaze to look just past Andy's shoulder. Her eyes widened in surprise as she looked directly into George's deep brown eyes.

'I'd settle for the last one,' he said in that deep voice she was becoming accustomed to.

Melody quickly put a dampener on the frisson of awareness his close proximity caused her. For a second she thought she'd spoken her last description out loud and lowered her gaze, forcing herself to concentrate on her work. She was almost ready to close.

'George,' she said, hoping her voice didn't betray the surprise, elation and confusion she felt at his unannounced presence. 'What brings you here?'

'Curiosity.'

'For compartment syndrome?'

He chuckled at her words and she momentarily allowed the sound to wash over her.

'Introduce us,' Andy whispered, and Melody cleared her throat.

'George, this is my registrar, Dr Andy Thompson, who is going to help me to close up Mr Potter's arm so we can get out of here.'

'Nice to meet you, Andy,' George remarked. Although he was wearing full theatre garb, George remained on the outer perimeter of the operating table.

'Likewise, sir.'

'Shouldn't that be "Sir Brilliant Surgeon"?' she teased Andy, as she started suturing.

'No. That was what *you* were supposed to call him,' Andy replied.

She glanced over at George. 'I take it coffee was served without a hitch?'

'Yes.'

'Good.' There was silence for a while as Melody and Andy continued with their work.

'It must have been a good night,' Andy said. 'At least, judging from Melody's flash hairstyle that's now hidden beneath her theatre cap.'

'It was,' George replied, his gaze meeting with Melody's for a few seconds.

'Right. We're done,' Melody announced, forcing herself to look away. She nodded to the anaesthetist before heading out of Theatre. She de-gowned and took a deep breath. George followed her, removing his own theatre garb as well. 'So why did you really come down here?' she asked as she headed into the doctors' tea room so she could write up the operation notes. When he didn't reply, she stopped and turned around, unsure whether he was still there. He collided with her, his hands instinctively resting on her waist to control his balance.

'Sorry,' she mumbled, and lifted her chin to gaze up at

him. They were standing just inside the door to the empty tea room and Melody didn't know whether she wanted it to fill up or stay deserted. 'I wasn't sure if you were…still…' Her voice trailed off. Aware that George hadn't removed his hands from her body, his touch burned through the green cotton of her theatre scrubs, making her intensely aware of their close proximity.

She felt a smouldering fire within her come to life. Her breathing became shallow, her lips parting to allow the air to escape. Her knees started to weaken as his thumb started moving in tiny circles, fanning the blaze.

His brown eyes were clouded with desire, his breathing as uneven as her own. 'Why did I really come?' he asked. They were close, so close that his breath fanned her cheek as he spoke. He smelled good—too good—and the scent of him only exacerbated the weakness of her knees. She knew she had to be careful, knew she had to keep control of her habit of jumping into the fire before assessing the risks. She'd been badly burned in relationships before and knew her inherent optimism of wanting to always see the best in people could get her into trouble. Was George Wilmont trouble? Was he married? Was he a widower? She still had no clue, and if it was the former then she wanted nothing to do with him, other than being the professional host the VOS required her to be.

'Melody, I…uh…' He paused and shook his head. 'I really didn't think this through,' he muttered, as he took a step away.

'Think what through?' She held her breath, her body zinging with anticipation. George was rattled and she secretly hoped it was *her* that had rattled him and even then, only because *he* had rattled her.

'Coming here. Walking into your theatre. Jabbering at you now.' He pushed a hand through his hair and shook his head. 'Sorry. This was a mistake.' He went to leave but turned when she called his name.

'Now that you're here, there is a question I want to ask you.'

'Oh?'

It was Melody's turn to feel awkward and unsure but after a moment of reflection she forged ahead. 'I'm sorry if this seems forward or overly personal but—are you married?'

He raised his eyebrows at the question. 'Married? No.'

A bubble of laughter rose in her and she momentarily covered her mouth. He wasn't married. This was a good thing, right? It meant that the feelings she was developing towards him weren't wrong, that she didn't need to feel any guilt at being attracted to him. 'Oh. It's in your dossier.'

'Really? You must have received an old copy of the information.' He glanced down at the floor for a moment before meeting her gaze once more. 'I'm a widower. My wife passed away eighteen months ago.'

'I'm sorry, George.' Her words were heartfelt.

'It wasn't your fault.'

'No, but losing someone close to you is never easy.'

He nodded. 'You'd think, seeing death as often as we do, that we'd have better coping mechanisms in place.'

'You'd think so, but it's rarely that cut and dried. It can take many years to get over a loved one's passing.'

'See?' He held one hand out towards her. 'That's exactly how I think. You...*get* me.' He sighed. 'Many people don't.'

'They expect you to move on with your life?'

He nodded. 'I know I'll have to—eventually—but...' He stopped.

'When you're ready, it'll happen.' Her words were soft. 'I haven't lost a spouse, but I have lost close friends and family. Grief takes time and that time is different for everyone.'

'Yes.' He raked a hand through his hair. 'And then you meet someone new and that person makes you…feel.'

'Feel what?'

'Just *feel*.' George shook his head. 'You made me *feel* today, Melody. That's what I've come here to tell you because I don't understand it and I didn't ask for it and… I just wanted to be open and honest and clear.'

'Clear? About what?' Feeling emboldened by their frank discussion, Melody took it one step further. 'That we're attracted to each other?'

'You feel it, too?' His words were soft, deep and filled with a mixture of confusion and longing.

'Yes.'

'Well… OK. Uh—I guess the next question is, do we do anything about it?'

'That *is* the question, and I don't know the answer.' She shrugged her shoulders.

George leaned against the bench and the two of them stared at each other. 'Neither do I.'

CHAPTER FIVE

LATER, AS MELODY drove home from the hospital, she reflected on the way she and George had just stared at each other, neither of them sure what to do or say next. They were attracted to each other and she was relieved they'd actually discussed this openly. Her past relationships had been riddled with lies.

So many lies. So many deceptions. So many mistakes. That's what her adult dating life had consisted of, which made George Wilmont's open frankness all the more appealing. It ran true to form that the next man to make her heart pound would be another unobtainable man, although thankfully not for the same cheating reasons as before.

George was single. George was devastatingly handsome. George lived over nine hundred kilometres away from her.

'It's just your luck in men,' she told herself as she opened the door to her apartment. She headed to her room and changed from the expensive evening gown into her comfortable pyjamas. It had been a long and hectic day, a day that would be seared in her memory for the rest of her life as it was the day she'd met George. She could clearly remember her father saying, 'Most days just run one into the other and then, out of nowhere, comes a day that can change your life for ever.'

'Oh, Dad,' Melody whispered. 'You were so right.' Her mind was full of mixed emotions—happiness, confusion, excitement and anticipation. What on earth would happen tomorrow? In order to wind her mind down from the hectic and tumultuous day, Melody headed to bed and pulled out the copy of her latest medical journal. She opened it to the paper she'd read the night before—a paper by Professor George Wilmont. Now that she'd met the man, when she re-read the paper she could hear his voice coming through the words on the page. That deep, sensual, melodious voice of his that was soothing and divine and…and that mouth as it moved to form words and…

When she almost dropped the journal on her face, Melody realised she was falling asleep. Putting the journal down beside her, she switched off the light and snuggled down, all too clearly recalling the way he could stand in front of a packed lecture room and enthral his audience. With visions of him in her head, she drifted off to sleep, a small smile on her lips.

The smile was still there the next morning as she awoke to her alarm with thoughts of George Wilmont still dancing around the edge of her dreams. She opened her eyes and stared at the ceiling. 'I dreamed about George.' She closed her eyes and turned off her alarm. How could she dream about a man she hardly knew? He was only here for another four days.

'Four days!' she told herself as she shoved the bed covers aside and headed to the bathroom. Turning on the shower taps, Melody allowed the spray of the hot water to calm her thoughts. 'You can do this,' she told her reflection as she dried her hair. 'You're a professional. Just go to the hospital, smile politely at him, do your work and just—just concentrate on—on…' She desperately thought of something else to think about before the answer hit. 'Your research.'

How had he managed to do it? Ever since Emir had broken her heart, ditching her for a life with another woman, Melody had focused solely on her work. True, being acting head of department was enough to keep her busy and she'd been grateful for that, but it still raised questions about her future.

Would she ever be a bride and not just a bridesmaid? Would she ever be a mother and not just an aunt? When would it be her turn? Would it *ever* be her turn? Had she missed her window? She wasn't getting any younger and her biological clock was definitely starting to tick. Was she just going to let two bad apples ruin what might be her opportunity to find a good apple? Could she risk her heart once again? Should she allow her fancy to have free rein or would George break her heart? If he did, where would she be then? Three times defeated by love!

Her thoughts continued to war as she finished getting ready for work, eating a light breakfast of juice and toast before driving to work. When she arrived, she made sure her cool, calm and collected professional façade was in place as she walked to her office. 'Good morning, Rick,' she said as she breezed in through the door.

'Well, hello. Aren't you looking like the consummate professional today?' her PA teased. She'd dressed in one of her power suits. Navy trousers and jacket and white silk shirt. Her hair was clipped back at her nape in the hope that her unruly curls would behave themselves.

'Thank you,' she replied as she quickly flicked through her in-tray. She had five minutes before she needed to head to the ward, so she dealt with some paperwork before returning the papers to Rick so he could process them.

'Gee, thanks,' he muttered, and she smiled sweetly at him. 'Off to ward round?'

'Yes.'

'Nervous?'

'Who, me?' she joked, and reached for her stethoscope. 'There's nothing else I have to do this morning? No more speeches? Introductions?'

'No. As far as George's schedule is concerned, he's accompanying you on the ward round and then he's back off to the lecture theatre. You're in clinic while he's lecturing to the fourth- and sixth-year medical students. Dinner this evening is at the hotel George is staying at.'

'Great. Thanks,' she said, then headed towards the ward. With every step she took, she did her best to calm her increasing nerves. She was going to see George again. Would she feel the same immediate connection as yesterday? Would it be stronger?

When she entered the ward, she felt as though she was going to be physically sick, her stomach was churning so much. It was ridiculous that simply the thought of seeing George was making her feel so nervous. Still, she took a deep breath and pushed open the door to the discussion room, where everyone congregated for the ward round meetings, only to find George and his team weren't there.

'Huh.' She couldn't help the deflation she felt. Why wasn't he here? Where was he? Were they still coming for her ward round?

Several medical students, interns, physiotherapists and nurses turned to look at her expectantly. Some murmured good morning, and Melody politely returned the greeting. There were more people than usual and she frowned, knowing it was due to George. Everyone wanted to learn, watch and absorb everything he did during his time there, and rightly so. It wasn't every day that visiting professors came to the hospital. It would make for a slower ward round, but it couldn't be helped. After all, this was a teaching hospital.

'There you are, Melody,' the CNC said as she came bustling in. 'I've just received a call from Rick, who wanted you to know Professor Wilmont and his team are stuck in traffic.'

Melody took a deep breath and let it out slowly, thinking fast. She was glad George and his team were OK and that nothing bad had happened to them. 'Thank you.' But what should she do now? Should she wait to see if George arrived within the next ten minutes or should she start the round without them? As a general rule, ward round started on time, regardless of who was or wasn't there. If ward round was late, it meant the catering and cleaning staff would be inconvenienced as it would interfere with their routines, the nursing staff would be running late all day and it also wasn't fair to the patients.

Melody followed the clinical nurse consultant back to her desk and reached for the phone. 'Rick?' she said a moment later. 'More information, please.'

'There's a car crash on Frost Road that's blocking traffic. Are you going to wait for them?'

'I'm not sure. Did Carmel give any more details?'

'She said they could be five minutes or five hours. She was sounding pretty stressed.'

'OK. We can't keep everyone waiting, and if George misses the entire ward round, he can just join tomorrow's, can't he?'

'Who are you trying to convince?' Rick laughed.

'Keep me informed of the situation.'

'Will do.'

Melody replaced the receiver. 'Thank you,' she said to the CNC. 'I'll be starting the ward round on time, Sister.'

'Of course, Doctor,' the CNC replied with a nod. Melody returned to the discussion room, where people were talking quite animatedly about the turn of events. She was swamped with questions as soon as she walked through the door.

'Is Professor Wilmont coming today or not?' one nurse asked.

'I have no idea. He's stuck in traffic. We'll be starting the round on time, though.'

'But you can't,' another complained.

'Yeah. This is my day off and I've specifically come in to watch him.'

'So have I.'

'I've cancelled a meeting,' someone else said.

'Well, I can't control peak-hour traffic any more than Professor Wilmont can,' Melody stated. This was not a good beginning to the day. 'We'll be starting the ward round in…' she glanced at her watch '…three minutes. Thank you.'

She walked out and headed to the ward kitchen. She needed coffee—and fast. She made herself half a cup and drank it down before returning to the discussion room to start the round. As they went from patient to patient, Melody kept checking the doorway, hoping George and his team would arrive.

They were halfway through the round when she looked up, straight into a pair of brown eyes that instantly melted her insides. George! His silent arrival threw her off guard and she faltered for a second but quickly managed to recover.

As they moved on to the next patient, Melody took the opportunity of announcing his presence. 'Glad you could finally make it, Professor Wilmont.' Several people turned to look at him. He merely nodded, not a smile in sight. 'I take it this morning's traffic jam will ensure you don't forget Sydney in a hurry,' she said lightly, and a few people chuckled. 'And now we come to Mrs Hammond. How are you this morning?' she asked her patient.

'Not bad, not bad, dearie. Got a bigger crowd than usual, I see.'

'Yes.' Melody smiled back and started her spiel on Mrs Hammond's injuries. Melody's stomach was knotted up again and she worked hard to control her involuntary emotional response to seeing George again. Yesterday hadn't been imagined. Her attraction to him was real. Very real.

After they'd finished the round, they returned to the discussion room, where Melody usually answered questions, as well as asking a few herself. She wasn't at all surprised when many people asked their questions of George and she was pleased when he checked with her before answering them.

Mindful of George's tight schedule, Melody checked her watch and called for a final three questions. He shot her a grateful look. Almost a minute later Carmel appeared in the doorway, ready to wrap things up.

As people starting filing out of the room, Carmel came up to her. 'I need to speak to you,' she said, her tone carrying a hint of annoyance, before she headed over to George. Melody wondered what on earth she'd done to annoy Carmel.

George was still talking to a few people and Melody needed to check on Mr Potter, who was still in the critical care unit under close supervision. 'I need to check on a patient and then I'll be in my office,' she told Carmel.

She nodded then politely interrupted George's conversation. Melody left, trying to figure out what was going on as she headed to CCU. Mr Potter's compartment syndrome was showing no signs of returning and Melody was pleased with his progress. He would need to have his drains taken out in a few days' time. She wrote up her notes, releasing Mr Potter back to the orthopaedic ward before heading to her office. No sooner had she sat in her chair than her door opened and an angry-looking Carmel stormed in.

'I wasn't at all impressed, Melody.'

'With what?' she asked, feeling her hackles begin to rise.

'You started the ward round without George!'

'What was I supposed to do? Wait for him?'

'He is the visiting orthopaedic surgeon,' Carmel pointed out.

'Who just happened to be stuck in a traffic jam. It wasn't my fault, Carmel. Besides, if it means that much to him, he can just come tomorrow.'

'But he was scheduled to come this morning.'

'And he did.'

'You still could have waited.'

'No, Carmel, I couldn't. Firstly, I have patients who are in hospital for treatment. That means physio and OT appointments. It means social workers calling on them. Time for their family and friends to visit. Meals need to be served. Blood tests and X-ray appointments need to be organised. If ward round is late then everything else is thrown off for the rest of the day. Secondly, I was also trying to keep to George's own schedule, which you're so rigid about adhering to.'

Carmel opened her mouth but Melody was all fired up. After all, she was a redhead and once she got going it was hard to stop her. 'Don't you even think of blaming me for this morning. I had no control over George being late, and just because you're angry and frustrated it doesn't mean you can look to me as your scapegoat. Accept the situation, Carmel. Accept that the ward round started without George.'

'But it was down on his schedule that he was to take the ward round.'

'*Take* the ward round? No. Your schedule was wrong. As far as I was concerned, George was merely *joining* my ward round. I'm in charge of that ward, Carmel. Not you, not George. If I'm away, the job falls to my senior registrar, Andy Thompson. As a visiting dignitary, surely George would realise that he has no real say in the treatment of my patients?'

'I do realise that,' George said from the doorway, and both Melody and Carmel turned to look at him. Neither of them had heard him enter and she wondered how long he'd been standing there. His words made her feel a little better but she was still angry with the way this entire morning had been handled.

'I'm glad to hear it,' she snapped.

'Why are you angry with me?' He spread his arms wide. 'Because you're the VOS. You know how ward rounds and hospitals work and, therefore, you should instruct your team accordingly.'

'You're right.' George crossed the room to stand next to them. 'Carmel, you promised me you'd be calm. Delays happen.'

'I *am* calm.' The words were said between clenched teeth and George couldn't help but smile. He placed a hand on his friend's shoulder. 'Diana was asking for your help in the lecture theatre. The Bluetooth isn't connecting properly today and one of the cables is missing.'

'Ugh!' Carmel growled. 'I *knew* today was going to be one of the bad days.' With that, George's PA stormed from the room.

'You'll have to excuse her. She's really a lovely person deep down inside but she's overly efficient, overly organised and overly obsessive-compulsive when it comes to schedules. A typical type A personality who doesn't know how to relax.'

Melody sighed, her earlier annoyance with Carmel dissipating. 'My brother used to be a type A personality. Then he survived a heart attack and changed his ways, thank goodness.'

He smiled. 'Thank you for understanding. It's been a very strange morning. Carmel had one of her hissy fits when I got out of the car to see if I could help. Thankfully, no one was badly injured so I returned to the car.' He tugged at the knot of his tie. 'Sometimes I wonder why I'm putting myself through this.'

'What? Wearing a tie?' she joked, hoping to lift the serious frown that now creased his brow. He stopped pacing and looked at her, the corners of his mouth twitching up slightly.

'You know what I mean. Just between you, me and the gatepost, I'm sick and tired of being handled all the time. It took a while to get used to and most of the time I can accept it, but on mornings such as these, when things are out of our control, Carmel goes off on one of her tangents.' George raked his hand through his hair and then shook his head. 'I probably shouldn't be talking to you about it. Sorry. I didn't mean to burden you with my problems.'

She didn't comment. She didn't want his confidences—they were too personal, and that was the last thing she needed, but who else did he have to talk to? 'Surely the professionalism between us can also extended to me offering my services as a sounding board?'

'Thank you.' He stared into her green eyes and she was glad she was still seated behind her desk as butterflies seemed to take flight in her stomach, twisting her emotions into nervous knots. How did he evoke such a reaction within her when she hardly knew him?

The tension between them was almost palpable, and it scared her. She didn't want this. She didn't want to become involved with a man who would be gone at the end of the week. Regardless of how he made her feel, he would leave and she would be left in limbo.

'I'd better go,' he said abruptly, breaking eye contact. Melody looked away as well, dragging in a deep breath.

'Yes.'

He walked over to the door and then stopped, turning to look at her. 'Are you coming up to the lecture theatre now?'

'Ah…' She stalled, knowing she should as his lecture was due to start within the next few minutes. 'I'll be along directly,' she told him.

Without another word, he left her office and Melody slumped forward over her desk. 'Why?' How was she supposed to find the strength to get through this week? No. She could do this. 'Pull yourself together,' she demanded. She tried to focus her thoughts on the work in front of her but her mind refused to budge from thoughts of George.

With one hypnotic glance, she was lost. He had a lovely smile, he had a great personality and he made her feel as though she was not only a woman of worth but also a woman of beauty. No man had ever made her feel that way before and that made George Wilmont different. The sensations he evoked were intensified, powerful and dynamic and that was very different from anything she'd felt before—*very* different.

CHAPTER SIX

'MELODY!' RICK'S VOICE made her spring up from her chair and glare at him standing by the door. 'You're supposed to be upstairs at the lecture.'

'How late am I?' How long had she been sitting there, thinking about George?

'It started ten minutes ago and the last thing I need is an angry text coming in from Carmel.'

'Carmel texted you asking where I was?'

'No.' Rick frowned. 'But I'm expecting one. That woman is crazy OCD when it comes to her scheduled events.'

'You can say that again,' Melody remarked as she shrugged into her suit jacket. 'I don't know why it should matter whether I'm a few minutes late. I'm not introducing him today. I'll just sneak in up the back and no one will notice.'

'George will,' Rick pointed out. 'He seems very...attentive towards you.' Her PA's tone was suggestive.

'He's just being a polite professional,' Melody countered.

'Ha! You should have seen him last night, pacing around with concern because you were late.' Rick waggled a finger at her. '*That* was not a polite or professional man.'

Melody sighed and shook her head. 'I don't have time to debate this with you.' As she headed out her office door, she pointed towards his desk. 'Do some...work stuff, will you?'

Rick chuckled and spread his arms wide. 'All done. This department is a well-oiled machine, thanks to me.'

Laughing at her PA's antics, Melody rushed to the lecture theatre, pushing Rick's comments from her thoughts and focusing on how best to sneak in. She didn't want George to think she wasn't interested in what he had to say because she was. When she arrived, he was just walking to the podium and she quickly sat down in one of the back seats. He looked up, his gaze melding with hers, as though he'd instinctively known where she was sitting, and her heart slammed wildly against her ribs.

Taking a breath, he began his talk, his gaze now roving over the audience before him. Melody found herself completely drawn in as he explained and illustrated, with the assistance of a detailed visual presentation, a new technique that could be adapted for both hip and knee arthroplasty. Afterwards, he was again inundated with questions and answered them patiently. He was brilliant. Handsome, successful, brilliant, and lived in a different city.

She should continue to recite that to herself over and over until Friday evening when her time with him would come to an end. George would leave here, just like all the other places, and she would do well not to let her thoughts have flights of fancy.

Melody returned to her office and collected her bag then headed to the restaurant across the street where they'd again be having lunch. This time there were only about thirty people, rather than the hullabaloo of yesterday, which meant they were in a smaller, more intimate function room.

'I didn't think you'd make it in time for the lecture but you did,' George commented as he sat down next to her, the warmth from his body, combined with his spicy aftershave, creating havoc with her senses.

'Sorry about missing the preamble.'

'No need to apologise. I thought an emergency might have come up after I'd left.'

'Nothing so justifiable. Just admin work.'

'Not your favourite, if I recall correctly.'

'I've learned if I keep on top of it, it isn't all that bad.'

'True.'

'Did you have to do a lot of admin work in your job prior to taking on the VOS?' Surely his work at Melbourne General Hospital was a safe topic. That way, she was finding out a bit more about him—but only in a professional capacity. She told herself that the questions she asked him should be the same questions she'd ask of any colleague and not just the colleague who was causing goose-bumps to pepper her skin at his nearness.

'I did. I was head of department, like you, but stepped down for these twelve months.' George leaned in closer to her and said in a conspiratorial whisper, 'And I'm not entirely sure I want to return.'

'Oh?' She tried not to stare at his mouth as he spoke. She tried to comprehend his words, the delicious scent he wore was creating havoc with her thoughts. 'To the hospital? To your job? To Melbourne?'

George stayed where he was for another moment, glancing at her mouth before meeting her gaze, causing another wave of delight to wash over her. Then he eased back in his chair, breathing in and sighing audibly, clearing his throat a little. 'I want to return to Melbourne, of course, and the hospital, but I'm not too sure about usurping the acting head as by all accounts he's doing an excellent job and...' George closed his eyes for a moment and shook his head. 'And I think I just need a break.'

'Understandable. The VOS is intensive and so is being head of a department.'

'Hmm.' He rubbed a hand over his chin, deep in thought. Melody watched him for another long moment, wanting to know his thoughts, wanting to be a sounding board for him, wanting to help him sort out this dilemma, but that wasn't her role. From the corner of her eye she saw that Carmel was headed their way and belatedly realised that while they'd been talking everyone else had taken their seats, the waiting staff already bringing out the entrées.

'Heads up,' she murmured, and George instantly looked towards where Carmel was almost upon them.

'Here's your next speech, George.' Carmel smiled encouragingly as she handed him some papers. 'There's no podium so—'

'Just stand and give it here?' he stated rhetorically and rose to his feet, putting the papers on the table in front of him and buttoning his jacket. As he did so, Melody reached for her water glass.

'Don't choke,' he said softly, giving her a wry smile.

'Funny,' she returned, just as softly, before he started his speech. She was impressed with the way he was able to make each speech sound unique and still provide interesting information on the chosen speciality of orthopaedics. Soon everyone was clapping and the rest of their meal was being served. The person seated to her left was a theatre nurse she'd worked with several times and the two of them talked about a variety of topics.

The entire time, she was acutely aware of George sitting on the other side of her, filling her water glass or offering her a bread roll or passing the butter. He was so attentive and yet everything he did seemed quite ordinary as he would often pass bread or butter to other people as well. Was she reading too much into every little thing? Every little move he made?

A few times she managed to share a moment of conversation with him, or join in the larger conversation going on around the table, but she couldn't shake the feeling that George was wanting to talk to her about something else, to continue their discussion about his position at Melbourne General or— Melody shook her head. She was going round the twist, trying to wrap her thoughts around the verbal and non-verbal conversations she and George were having. What she *was* completely conscious of, though, was the way just being next to him was increasing her awareness of him. How was she supposed to get the man out of her head when her body seemed to be tuning itself to his frequency?

Just as coffee was being served, Melody checked her watch and gasped when she realised the time.

'Something wrong?' George asked, a frown on his face.

'If I don't hustle, I'll be late for clinic.' She took a quick sip of her coffee.

'I'll walk back with you,' he stated.

'That's not necessary.' She drained her cup and stood. 'Besides, it will take you ages to get out of here. Everyone wants to have a word with you.'

'Well, they'll have to wait. I need to have a word with *you.*'

'Oh.' Melody wasn't quite sure what to say. She shifted away from the table and pushed her chair in as the nurse who'd been sitting beside her asked George a question. Melody watched as George turned from her and gave the nurse his attention, but instead of listening intently he actually fobbed the nurse off.

'I'm sorry, I have an important meeting and I'm running late. Will you be at the dinner tonight?'

The nurse nodded.

'How about we catch up then?'

'Sounds great,' the nurse replied, her eyes saying that she'd like to do more than just talk with him. George, however, seemed oblivious of the nurse's intentions. It made Melody wonder whether George was a bit of a player, like Emir. She had no real reason to believe anything he said. She'd only met the man yesterday and already he'd told her that he was attracted to her. Wasn't that odd? Sure, he'd be gone by the end of the week but perhaps his entire plan was to enjoy a night or two of hot, meaningless sex with her before he left. She had no idea.

As she left the room where they'd had lunch, she saw Carmel noticing George was trying to leave early. Chances were that Carmel would stop him from leaving and if Melody waited, it would make her even later for clinic. She was out of the restaurant and heading towards the pedestrian crossing when George caught up with her.

'I thought I said I'd walk back with you.'

'From the look of things, you were otherwise engaged.'

'What are you talking about?'

'Forget it,' she said, angry with him for not knowing when women were throwing themselves at him. Surely an attractive man of his age knew how to reel in the females? She shook her head. He was no different from Emir. Emir, who'd had affairs with far too many female staff members at the hospital. Emir, who'd had such an easy, charming manner with women and used it to his best advantage. Well, she wasn't going to be taken in by another womaniser.

'So what did you want to talk about?' she asked as the pedestrian light turned green. She headed off across the road with George at her side, both equally as huffy as the other.

'I wanted to talk about what's going on between us.'

'What? Now?' She spread her arms wide as she crossed to the other side of the main road. 'George, we're both a little busy.' She pointed to the restaurant. 'Go back and do your job and leave me to do mine.'

'Wait. Why are you angry with me again?'

Melody opened the side door leading to a staircase that came out near her office. George followed her, their footsteps echoing off the walls. When they came out in the department, she headed up the corridor and went directly into her office. She held the door for him and closed it the instant he was inside.

'What is it that you couldn't wait to tell me?' she asked.

George didn't stop walking and paced restlessly around her office. 'Well, now I feel stupid with what's just happened and how—' He stopped and raked a hand through his hair, then looked at her for a long moment. 'You get in my head, Melody.'

'Huh?'

'Last night at the dinner, today at the lecture, just now at lunch—you get in my head and turn my thoughts to mush, and that's not good.'

'What are you talking about?'

He covered the distance between them with a few easy strides, then slipped his arms around her waist, bringing her closer. 'Do you feel that?'

The heat of his body? The spicy scent surrounding him? The way such a touch could cause her body to come instantly to life, so much so that she forgot all rational thought? 'Y-yeah.'

'That's what I'm talking about. You're in my head and I can't think straight when I'm near you, so I think to myself, Look, George, just keep your distance. Be professional. But then when I'm not around you, I'm thinking—about—you.' As he spoke the last two words, his gaze dipped to once more encompass her mouth. 'I think about kissing you. I think about holding you like this—and so much more.'

Melody closed her eyes against the heady combination he was presenting. 'I know.' She needed to think clearly, to say what she needed to say. 'But how am I supposed to know you don't give this spiel to every woman you meet in a new town? You'll be gone at the end of the week and I'll probably never see you again.' She opened her eyes after speaking the words, wondering if he was listening to what she was saying or whether he was just intent on following the physical attraction between them.

'And I keep thinking that you might be the sort of woman to bewitch every man you meet. How am I supposed to know that you don't flirt with every new surgeon

you meet? Or whether you really do like me for who I am—
underneath the pomp and ceremony of the title—because,
believe me, I've seen it all.'

'Have you?' Melody eased back slightly and George immediately dropped his arms.

'You'd be surprised.' George slumped down into the
chair and sighed heavily. 'I guess for some people sex is
just sex. It isn't linked with emotions or consequences, but
for me, well, I'm afraid it comes with both.'

'So you never took anyone up on their…offer?' She
walked around her desk and sat in her chair.

George met her gaze and slowly shook his head. 'I
haven't been interested in anything but work—until yesterday morning when I met you.'

'Oh.' Again, there was that honesty. He was being as
open and as forthcoming as he'd been last night when she'd
finished in surgery. Both of them were clearly perplexed
by this instant and mutual attraction yet both of them also
knew it was pointless to give in to their feelings. However,
when George held her the way he was, Melody had a difficult time remembering anything to do with rational thinking. 'I guess that does change things.'

'It does, Melody. It really does and I have this overwhelming urge to tell you about my life, to share my
thoughts and concerns with you.'

'Such as whether or not to take up your previous position when you return?'

'Well, that and—and I want to tell you about my life,
about the things that matter to me, about what movies I like,
about what makes me laugh and—and about—my wife.'

'Your wife?' She was surprised at this.

'Yes. You see, the way you make me feel—which I had
never expected to feel again—is making me question everything.'

'It is?'

'Yes.' He buried his face in his hands for a moment before standing to pace once more. 'Look, I'll just blurt it out because chances are, as I sneaked away from the lunch without Carmel's permission, she'll be calling me in a minute to tell me I'm late for my next appointment. Also, you have clinic so— Right.' He stopped pacing and shoved his hands into his pockets. 'I'll just come out and say it.'

'OK.'

'My wife, Veronique was her name.' He paused and looked down at the floor, clenching his jaw. A moment later he lifted his head and met her gaze. 'She was my admin assistant for about a year before we were married. It was her idea to apply for the VOS and, in fact, when I was successful in obtaining the post, Veronique was the one who arranged everything.' He clenched his jaw then forced himself to relax before saying softly, 'She died in a road accident six months before the VOS began.'

'She was supposed to be with you on this tour? In Carmel's job?' Melody sighed and nodded, realising how difficult things must have been for him.

'Yes. We were supposed to be experiencing all of this together. She was proud of me and my work and she wanted the world to know about it.' He shoved his hands into his pockets again. 'After she passed away, I felt I owed it to her to do the tour, to carry out her wishes, as it were.' He shook his head sadly. 'Obligation, eh? It makes us do things we don't want to.'

'Your wife was right to be proud of you and to want the rest of the world to know about your techniques and the device you've invented. Obligation or not, the VOS will help so many surgeons to perfect their techniques and, in turn, will help their patients and that, George, is very noble. *You* are noble.'

'No.' He shook his head for emphasis. 'I'm far from it because what man has these sorts of feelings for another woman eighteen months after his wife's death?' He gestured to the two of them. 'That's not noble. That's not respectful. That's not the type of legacy I want to leave to Veronique.'

His words were raw and painfully honest and it allowed Melody see that the man before her was still a man very much in love with his wife. He may have feelings for her but they were clearly feelings he didn't understand and neither did she. Both of them were trying to make some sort of sense of this undeniable instant attraction they felt for each other.

His phone rang and he sighed heavily when he saw the caller.

'Carmel?' she asked.

He nodded and connected the call, not bothering to say hello but just listening before saying, 'I'll be right there.' He disconnected the call and put his phone back into his pocket. 'Duty calls.'

'For both of us,' she added, as she crossed to the coat rack near her door and picked up her white clinic coat. George, the gentleman that he was, took the coat from her and helped her into it before passing her the stethoscope from her desk. 'Thank you for being honest.' She angled her head to the side and smiled. 'It's refreshing.'

'Thank *you* for listening to me ramble and I don't mean to scare you or confuse you any further but I wanted you to know—' He stopped and raked both hands through his hair. 'I'm probably not making any sense.'

'Yes. Yes, you are, George. In telling me about Veronique, in sharing what this tour meant to both of you, it might help us both to put the brakes on these crazy feelings we're having.'

'Exactly.' He shook his head. 'But when you say things like that, when you *understand* what it is I'm trying to say, that only makes it worse because it highlights just how well you seem to know me and that only intensifies the attraction I feel for you, because the last woman who understood me the way you instinctively do was—'

'Veronique,' she finished for him.

'Yes.' He stared at her for another fifteen seconds then turned and opened her office door. 'We're both going to be late if we stand here trying to make any sense out of this.'

'True. Work. Work is always dependable.'

'Work will see you through.' He followed her out of the office and waited while she locked her door. 'It's what I told myself after Veronique's death.'

'Yeah. It's what I told myself after my break-ups.' She smiled sadly at him. 'Have fun at your next meeting.'

'Have fun at clinic,' he stated, then grinned. 'Ah—clinic. Those were the quiet and uncomplicated days of my past.'

She laughed, pleased they'd been able to lighten the atmosphere a bit. 'You sound nostalgic.'

'I am.' He pointed to the stairwell door. 'I'm going this way.'

She pointed towards the direction of clinic. 'And I'm going this way.'

'Will you be at the dinner tonight?'

'Yes.'

'See you then.'

With that, she turned and walked away from him, proud of herself when she didn't look back. George Wilmont had just provided her with another reason why she needed to keep away from him—the fact that he'd clearly adored his wife. 'And that only makes him more attractive,' she grumbled as she headed into clinic, apologising to the sister for her tardiness.

She did her best to push thoughts of George and everything he'd told her to the back of her mind so she could concentrate on clinic. Thankfully, with the back-to-back patients she hardly had time to draw breath let alone dwell on thoughts relating to George. She managed to finish seeing all her patients just after five-thirty, which was only half an hour late. Melody wrote up the last of the notes as her registrar, Andy, stopped by to let her know he was also finished. 'Are you coming to the dinner tonight?' she asked.

'After missing last night's dinner? I'll definitely be there.'

'See you there.' She returned her attention to the notes but heard Andy's voice in the distance, talking to someone. The nurses had left the instant the last patient had departed so Melody wondered who it might be. Seconds later, she heard footsteps heading towards her consulting room and looked up expectantly at the open doorway.

'Hi,' George said a moment later. 'I hope I'm not disturbing you?'

Melody's heart lurched happily at the sight of him and a shiver of excited anticipation worked its way down her spine. Yes, he was disturbing her—far too much for her liking. 'No. I'm just finishing up.' She motioned to the notes, all the while trying to calm the effect he was having on her.

'Don't let me interrupt,' he said, and looked at some of the posters stuck up on the wall around the clinic room. Melody quickly finished writing the notes and the instant she'd closed the file and put her pen down, the phone on the desk rang.

'Excuse me,' she said, but George merely nodded. 'Dr Janeway.'

'Oh, Melody. Good, I caught you. An emergency has just come in. They're demanding the head of unit,' the triage sister said.

Melody groaned resignedly. 'Details?'

'Right scapula, right Colles' and dislocation of the neck of humerus. Melody, it's Rudy Carlew.'

'Is that name supposed to mean something to me?'

'Honestly, Melody, don't you ever go to the movies?'

'Sure. So?' She glanced at George only to find him watching her.

'Problem?' he asked softly.

'Emergency,' she mouthed, and he nodded.

'Rudy Carlew is the hottest thing in movies,' the triage sister was saying. 'Mr Gorgeous? *Everybody's Hero*? That's the latest superhero movie—surely you've seen that one?'

'Oh, yeah. I've seen that one. Right.' Melody at least had a picture of the actor in her head.

'He's been filming his latest film in several locations around Sydney and today they were doing a stunt, and he fell.'

'OK. I'm on my way.' She hung up the receiver and turned her attention to George.

'What's happening?'

'Rudy Carlew is in the ED.'

'Who?'

Melody laughed. 'I'm glad to see I'm not the only one out of touch. He's a movie star,' she continued as she packed up her desk and headed for the door. Turning out her light, she looked over her shoulder at him. 'Want to accompany me to the ED?'

'Sure.' His enthusiasm was evident.

'I guess most of the operating you've done has been scheduled, right?'

'Exactly. I can't recall the last time I dealt with an emergency.'

Melody pressed the button for the lift and while they waited she tilted her head and eyed him thoughtfully. 'What's the deal with your operating and practising licence? You must have operated in some of the finest facilities in the world.'

'I have. For visiting professorships, the recipient is granted an international operating licence.'

'So you could quite easily operate with me right now if I asked?'

'Yes.' The lift arrived and they rode it to down to the ED. 'Will you?' George asked the question with the delighted anticipation of a child at Christmas. 'Please?'

Melody couldn't help but smile at him. 'I don't know.'

She pretended to consider him thoughtfully. 'How's your upper-limb expertise?'

'Pretty rusty,' he confessed. 'But I'd only be assisting,' he was quick to point out.

'Let's see how his injuries present. Chances are he won't require surgery at all.' She told him what the triage sister had said and he nodded, all pretence gone as they walked into the ED. If she'd wanted to get people's attention, she had it—walking in with the visiting orthopaedic surgeon to treat a movie star.

What had started out as a difficult day was turning into one that most definitely had its perks.

CHAPTER SEVEN

THE NOISE COMING from outside was deafening and hospital security was stationed at the front door, as well as the door that led through to the treatment area.

'Oh, there you are, Melody,' the triage sister said, a hint of excitement mixed with exasperation in her voice. 'He's in treatment room two.'

'Thanks.' Melody pointed to where the security guards were standing. 'What's going on?'

'Mr Carlew's fans!'

'Oh.' Melody shrugged and led the way to treatment room two. 'Hello,' she said to the patient lying on the bed. She did indeed recognise the talented Rudy Carlew. 'I'm Dr Janeway, Head of Orthopaedics. This is my colleague, Professor Wilmont.'

Rudy Carlew nodded slightly and then winced in pain.

'Can't you people do something?' the woman standing next to him complained. 'He's in pain.'

Melody accepted the patient chart from one of the nurses and checked his analgesics. 'Are you still experiencing pain, Mr Carlew?'

'Rudy,' he said softly.

'Any pain, Rudy?'

'Minor.'

'You people have got to do something,' the woman shrilled again.

'I don't believe we've been introduced.' Melody politely.

The woman sighed with dramatic exasperation. 'I'm his manager. Now do something.'

'I will,' Melody said. 'Unfortunately, you'll need to wait outside. The sister here will show you where.'

'I'm not leaving him.' The woman grabbed his hand and poor Rudy cried out in pain.

'It's all right, Astrid. I'll be in good hands.'

Astrid looked at him, then back to the doctors. 'He's worth a lot of money to the studio, so fix him.'

'Why don't you appease the fans, Astrid,' Rudy stated.

'Yes. I can do that.' Astrid headed out.

'Now, Rudy.' Melody moved in for a closer look at his injuries. 'Let's see what sort of damage has been done.' She inspected both his arms gently. He had a few cuts and scratches on his legs and upper torso, which had been attended to by the ED staff.

'I think we'll let Radiology enjoy your company next.' Melody smiled as she wrote up the X-ray request forms. 'You've dislocated your shoulder but I don't want to put it back in without it being X-rayed first.'

'Why not?' he asked.

'Because you may have fractured the top of your humerus, which is the upper arm bone. If you have, we'll need to operate in order to fix the pieces of bone together before we can even attempt a relocation.'

'If not?'

'Then I can put it back in.'

'Will it be painful?

Melody smiled. 'We'll make sure you have sufficient analgesics to cover the pain. Your Colles' fracture, which is your wrist, looks straightforward and can probably be fixed with a simple plaster cast.'

'I can't have a cast on my arm,' he stated in a normal voice. 'I'm right in the middle of shooting a movie. The hold-up of waiting for my arm to heal in a cast would cost the studio millions.'

'I'm sure we can arrange for you to have your arm strapped and then in a half-cast for the hours when you're not on camera.' Melody continued calmly. 'There are options.'

'Can I get a second opinion?'

'Of course,' she replied, not at all offended. 'First of all, let's see what the X-rays show and then we'll know exactly what we're dealing with.'

'Right you are, Doc,' he said with a smile. He was a handsome man, Melody thought, but his looks were too... *polished*.

'You handled that well,' George said once Rudy had been wheeled off, with three adoring nurses at his side, towards Radiology.

'Why do you sound so surprised?' She laughed as she led him into the ED tea room. 'Coffee?'

'Thanks,' he said as he took off his suit jacket and loosened his tie.

'Black. No sugar, right?'

'How did you know?'

Melody chuckled. 'Let's see, since you arrived here, I've already had three meals sitting next to you. I simply noticed you didn't add anything into your coffee before you drank it.'

He smiled at her. 'And you have yours with just milk.'

'I do.' Melody quickly fixed them coffee and brought the cups over to the lounge where he was sitting. George took a sip of his coffee, then put the cup on the small table in front of them. He stretched his arms over his head and closed his eyes.

'How long do you think Rudy will be in Radiology?'

Melody knew that George had said something but for the life of her she had no idea what he'd said because her gaze had been drawn to the way his muscles flexed beneath his shirt when he stretched. It should be outlawed. His crisp, white shirt did nothing to hide what lay beneath and Melody's heart rate accelerated.

She quickly looked away, in case he intercepted her gaze. What was she doing, ogling him like that? He was a man in love with another woman. Or, more correctly, the *memory* of another woman. Memories were powerful things to compete with. She stopped her thoughts short. Wait. Compete? Did she *want* to compete for George's attention?

'Melody?' There was concern in his voice when he spoke.

'Sorry.' She forced herself to meet his gaze but she didn't hold it for long. She needed to be careful. She'd been burned too often in the past and perhaps it was necessary for her to remind herself every day that soon George would leave her life just as quickly as he'd entered it. Besides, did she really want to risk a quick fling with a man when she'd vowed to take the next relationship slowly—*very* slowly? She glanced his way again and found him watching her.

'Something wrong?'

'No. No. Nothing's wrong.' She shook her head for emphasis and then eyed him cautiously. 'Why do you ask?'

'No reason,' he stated. 'You just seemed miles away.'

'Hmm.' She tapped the side of her head. 'There's a lot going on up here but nothing I'll burden you with.' She chattered too fast, which indicated how his nearness was starting to affect her. She should stand, she should move, she should put more distance between them as right now the warmth and charm exuding from him was starting to become like an aphrodisiac to her. What was wrong with her? She was behaving like an adolescent with a crush.

It certainly didn't help matters when he shifted closer and leaned towards her. 'This attraction between us...' he murmured quietly, his gaze holding hers.

'Hmm?' Melody waited, holding her breath to see what he would say next.

'I try to stop myself but then I get near you and...' He paused. 'Are you...seeing anyone at the moment?' He wasn't sure why he was asking. Perhaps it was because her earlier comment about relying on work to help her through after her break-ups had made him think. Although they both knew that nothing should happen between them, he still seemed to have a burning need to know all about her.

'Uh...' That wasn't what she'd expected him to say but the fact that he'd asked her that particular question meant— what? What did it mean? That he was hoping something was going to happen between them? That he was check- ing—just in case? 'Actually, no. I'm not involved with any- one. My...er...my last relationship didn't end well.'

'I'm sorry to hear that.' And his words were genuine, which surprised her.

'You are?'

He shrugged one shoulder and shifted again, sliding one arm down the back of the lounge, his hand now resting near her back. 'Everyone deserves to find happiness, Melody.'

'True but I—' She shrugged. 'I guess happiness keeps eluding me.'

'Was it serious?'

'We were engaged.'

She'd been engaged? The thought had never crossed his mind. It also drove home just how little he knew about her. 'Does he work here?'

'No. He did, though. Thankfully, he left and moved to Germany.'

'That's a big move.'

'Well—given the doctor he impregnated while cheating on me lives in Germany, it was logical.' Melody couldn't hide the pain she felt at Emir's betrayal.

'What a fool.'

'To move to Germany?'

'No. To cheat on *you*.'

'Oh.'

'You deserve better than that.'

'I do, don't I?' She met his gaze, her eyes flicking to encompass his very near, very kissable mouth. She closed her eyes, needing to control her increasing attraction to him. 'But it's made me very cautious, George.' She opened her eyes and stared into his.

Neither of them moved. Both were caught in the bubble of sensual awareness that only seemed to intensify every time they were alone.

The tea-room door opened and a nurse poked her head around. George instantly stood and picked up his coffee cup, carrying it to the sink. 'Rudy Carlew's films are available for viewing,' she stated, pointing to the computer in the corner of the room.

'Thanks.' As soon as the door closed, Melody sighed and looked at him. 'Fast moves.'

'I'm too old for this and—I don't want anyone to think there's anything going on between us.'

'There isn't.'

'But the gossips make up their own stories based on little fact.'

'You're worried about the gossips?' She stood and headed over to the computer, entering her code so they could view the X-rays.

'I am.' He shook his head. 'It's not fair to you.'

Wow. Was he really that concerned about her? How incredibly sweet. She smiled warmly and beckoned him over. 'The dislocation of the shoulder looks clean,' she said as he joined her. He wasn't as close as he'd just been and for that she was grateful. She needed to concentrate and she was finding it increasingly difficult to do so with George around. She clicked on the next image. 'Ulna and radius, on the other hand, not so clean. It'll require open reduction and internal fixation.'

'You'll need to reduce and relocate the Colles' as well,' George pointed out. 'What do you think about bandaging and putting his arm in a splint?'

'We just need to keep everything stable,' she agreed with a nod.

'If you insert a few K-wires here…' George pointed up to the fracture site of Rudy Carlew's right wrist '…that will hold the fracture in place.'

'I'd need to restrict him in the length of time he is out of the splint and he'll require a nurse to handle the bandaging.'

'Absolutely.'

'What do you think? An hour a day.'

'At least for the first two weeks. Then once you get the check X-rays done, you may be able to extend that time frame or decrease it, depending on how things look.'

Melody nodded. 'Could be a workable solution. Let's see how we go in Theatre. And speaking of which…' She walked to the phone on the wall and called through to the emergency theatres to see if one could be booked immediately.

'We're in luck,' she told him as she finished putting in the verbal request. Next she headed back to her patient, who was now in one of the isolated rooms at the end of the recovery cubicles.

'It looks as though we may have a solution to your problem,' Melody told Rudy. 'But,' she added at his brilliant smile, 'you'll be under strict instructions as to how much you can do and, please, no more stunts! Use the stuntman next time.'

'Yes, Doctor,' Rudy said with mock remorse.

'I can't make any promises,' Melody reiterated. 'It was Professor Wilmont's idea so if it doesn't work out, you can blame him for dashing your hopes.'

George chuckled. Melody explained the operation to Rudy and once he'd signed the consent form, she headed to Theatre to get everything prepared. 'It's six-thirty now,'

Melody said to him. 'Unfortunately, it doesn't look as though you'll have time to help me in Theatre.'

'Why not?'

'George, you have a dinner at eight o'clock. That's only an hour and a half away.'

'I do know how to tell the time,' he said with an admonishing grin.

'Stop teasing.' Melody smiled, enjoying their easy banter. Emir had never clicked with her like this. Perhaps that was why she found George so hard to resist! 'Carmel will come looking for you and then you'll have to leave in the middle of the operation. Actually, I'm surprised she's allowed you a few free hours.'

George chuckled. 'It'll be all right. The operation's going to take—what? Forty-five minutes?'

'More than likely, if we don't run into complications.'

'I seriously doubt it.'

'You have responsibilities.'

'I have an hour and a half. We'll be fine.'

The look he gave her said that she could trust him and for a split second Melody wondered whether he was only talking about the operation or—something more? She decided it was best not to pursue it so she showed him where the changing rooms were and escaped behind the door marked 'Females'.

'You're a cool, calm and collected professional,' she mumbled to herself as she changed. 'You've been through a lot worse than this. It's just an attraction. Nothing is ever going to come of it. He's still carrying a torch for his wife and he's leaving at the end of the week. He has a tour to complete and even after that's done he'll be living in a different state.'

'Talking to yourself again, Melody?' Evelyn asked as she walked in to the changing rooms.

For a second she froze. How much of her mumbling had

Evelyn heard? Melody adopted an air of nonchalance and continued to put her hair up.

'So, another opportunity to work with the great Professor Wilmont,' Evelyn squeaked excitedly. 'And assist with an operation on Rudy Carlew. Is this the best job or what?'

Melody couldn't help but laugh. She didn't need to tell Evelyn to make sure she kept herself the information about Rudy Carlew strictly confidential as the nurse had proved herself to Melody in the past to be a woman of integrity and discretion. If it hadn't been for Evelyn's compassion in telling Melody the truth about Emir, perhaps Melody's heartbreak would have been even worse.

'The only downside,' Evelyn continued, 'is that after tonight my contract with the hospital expires.'

'I didn't realise you were doing agency work. You've been here for at least the past twelve months.'

'I've been filling in for a nurse on maternity leave. She's back tomorrow, which means I won't be around to visit Rudy.' They walked out together. 'How did you get Professor Wilmont to agree to operate?'

Evelyn's question made Melody want to throw caution to the wind and say something like it had been her natural charms that had led George away from his busy schedule in search of a more refined amusement but instead she cleared her throat. Not wanting to create hospital gossip, she said, 'Firstly, he's *assisting* me. Secondly...' Melody shrugged '...he asked.'

Melody checked on Rudy to make sure that everything was going according to plan before she headed for the scrub sink. There was no sign of George but she knew he'd arrive soon. The hairs on the back of her neck and along her arms rose the moment he entered the room and she was amazed at how aware she was of him but tried to hide it as best she could.

As they stood at the scrub sink, he said, 'Everything ready to go?'

'Yes.'

'I called Carmel,' he told her. 'So at least she knows where I am.'

Melody glanced at him and almost gasped. The theatre greens brought out the golden flecks in his brown eyes—eyes that she could willingly drown in. She tried not to dwell on it and scrubbed her hands harder but the scent of his aftershave, the deep melodious sound of his voice, the warmth emanating from his body as he stood beside her made her completely forget what she was doing. She glanced at his large, capable hands as he continued to lather them and his arms. So strong. So masterful. So…sensual.

This will not do! Melody returned her gaze to her own arms and hands, intent on focusing her thoughts on the up-coming operation. Thankfully, by the time the operation began she was back in control of her emotions. George was merely another surgeon assisting her.

They worked well together, relocating the shoulder and performing open reduction and internal fixation on the fractured radius and ulna. The K-wires that needed to be inserted into the wrist were another matter yet together they worked it through with both of them quite satisfied with the result.

'A job well done,' George remarked as he pulled off his mask and theatre cap. Melody looked up at him and he smiled. It was that gorgeous thousand-watt smile that sent her body into meltdown. A flood of tingles swamped her, and her knees turned to jelly.

She turned away from him, desperate to get herself under control. She had to find some way of saving her sanity, at least for the next few days, but the more time she spent with George, the more she was coming to care for him and that in itself was incredibly dangerous.

CHAPTER EIGHT

'MELODY? ARE YOU feeling all right?'

'Yes.' She dared a quick glance up at him while she disposed of her theatre garb. 'I'd better write up the notes,' she mumbled, and quickly headed back to the tea room, thankful George wasn't following her.

She was glad of the momentary reprieve as it gave her a moment to get her racing heart rate under control. She wrote up the notes but discovered she'd made two mistakes. It irked her when her mind wandered into George-land. Why *did* it irk her so much? Was it the fact that she was attracted to George? Or the fact that she felt out of control whenever he was around? And what was wrong with feeling a little out of control once in a while?

She knew there could never be anything between them so why shouldn't she enjoy the way he made her pulse race? Or the way her stomach churned in excitement? It was definitely bolstering her bruised ego. George found her desirable. After what Emir had done to her, why shouldn't she be delighted with George's attentions? It could be something she could hold close to her heart, especially when she became all anxious about never finding anyone to truly love and accept her.

'Thought I'd find you here.' George's voice washed over her and Melody momentarily closed her eyes, savouring the sound and the way it made her feel, before opening her eyes and turning to look at him. He was dressed in his suit again, looking more handsome than before, if that was possible. 'I'd better get going.' He stayed in the doorway, not venturing any further.

Melody automatically looked at the clock, gasping as she saw the time. Ten minutes to eight. 'I'd completely forgotten about the dinner.'

He smiled. 'I thought as much. You are still coming?'

'Yes, but it appears I'm going to be a little late. As the dinner is at your hotel, it won't take you anytime at all to change and get to the venue.'

'Whereas you need to go home, shower and change and then drive to the hotel,' he finished for her.

'Yes.'

'I'll save you a seat.'

Melody chuckled. 'That's pretty decent of you—especially as the seating has already been assigned.'

He returned her smile and she melted. 'See you there,' he said, then walked away. Melody sighed, the silly smile still on her face. You're not having much luck, she rationalised. Even though she knew George still carried a torch for his wife, she couldn't blame him. To have loved and then lost would mean that Veronique would be in his heart for ever. The problem was that it only endeared him to her even more. He wasn't about to let his past fade away but would carry those memories with him for ever. But was he looking to move forward? To try new relationships? He said it had been only eighteen months since his wife had died, so was he ready, and did it really have anything to do with her?

'Work,' she said, and stood, pushing thoughts of George Wilmont out of her mind. She headed for Recovery to check on Rudy and when she was satisfied with his condition, she left the nurses to drool over their movie-star patient.

* * *

At home, she took a leisurely shower and dressed with extra care. She'd seen the slightly veiled looks of desire in George's eyes yesterday evening, and tonight she wanted to see it again. He made her feel feminine, delicate and sexy—all at the same time. They were sensations she'd never felt before and she'd discovered, much to her chagrin, that she liked it.

Melody smoothed her hand down the long burgundy silk dress she'd bought two weeks ago specifically for this occasion. Tonight, instead of piling her curls on top of her head, she let them fall loose. Vanilla essence was next and she dabbed some on her wrists and behind her ears. Usually, she wore perfume but tonight she wanted to—what? Leave a lasting impression on George? Have him find her too good to resist?

'Just enjoy it,' she told her reflection. 'Nothing is going to happen and at least you'll have some nice memories to combat the awful ones.' With a firm nod, she collected her bag and keys before heading out the door.

Melody arrived just over an hour later, but when George saw her he knew it had been worth the wait. The same reaction he'd experienced the night before hit him again. She was a vision of loveliness, dressed in a rich burgundy fabric that shimmered when she walked. Her hair was loose and he had the sudden urge to thread his fingers through her glorious mane that shone reddish-gold beneath the artificial lights. He was amazed at how strongly she affected him and although he'd done his best to fight it, he'd found he was losing the battle.

'Hey. Here's Melody,' Andy announced, breaking into George's intimate thoughts. George watched her look their way as Andy called her name and waved. She waved back and said something to the people who had waylaid her before heading in their direction. She walked with such grace and poise, holding her shoulders back. She was one elegant lady.

George waited impatiently for their gazes to meet and when they did he found it hard to disguise the desire he felt. He smiled quickly, hoping she hadn't seen, but he doubted it. Even though he'd only met her yesterday morning, George knew she was a very perceptive woman.

He stood and held the back of the vacant chair next to him. 'Here, have a seat. You must be exhausted.'

'Thank you.'

'How did the operation go?' Andy asked from across the round table.

'Routine,' Melody replied. 'How did you know?'

'George said you'd been called to Theatre. So it was nothing interesting?'

'Not really. Dislocated shoulder, fractured ulna, radius and Colles'.'

'Sports injury?'

'No. Actually, the patient sustained a fall.' As she spoke, George motioned to the waiter, who nodded in understanding and soon brought out a meal for Melody.

'I had the kitchen hold a meal for you. I knew you'd be hungry after being in clinic and then Theatre,' he told her when she looked at him with delighted surprise.

'That's so considerate. Thank you, George.' His thoughtfulness touched her deeply. How was she supposed to resist him when he did such nice things? 'I thought I might have missed out.'

'I knew you'd be hungry,' he told her softly, delighted that he'd impressed her. He felt himself preen like a peacock and couldn't stop it. 'After all, you've been going nonstop since lunchtime.'

'I'm famished,' she agreed, and tucked right in. He was pleased to see she had a healthy appetite and didn't appear concerned about her figure. Veronique had been the same. In fact, Melody had many of the same qualities as

Veronique and in a strange way it comforted him. Perhaps that was the reason he'd been drawn to Melody in the first place.

As far as looks went, they were like chalk and cheese. Veronique had been a bit shorter than Melody, who he guessed to be about five feet eight inches. Where Melody had long auburn hair, Veronique's had been blonde and short. Melody had green eyes, Veronique's had been brown.

Yet a lot of their mannerisms were very similar. The way they walked. The intelligence, which was reflected in their eyes, and the way they could both make him laugh. It was uncanny and nerve-racking at the same time. The main difference he could see was that Melody was a surgeon and, therefore, understood every aspect of his work. That hadn't always been the case with his wife. The simple delight he'd felt standing at the operating table by Melody's side, assisting her with a routine procedure, had surprised him. The knowledge made him feel guilty, as though he was cheating on Veronique because he could share a part of his life with Melody that he hadn't been able to completely share with his wife.

Melody was a giving, caring and open person, just as Veronique had been. It stood to reason that he'd be attracted to a woman with similar qualities, but where his feelings for Veronique had grown over time, his immediate awareness of Melody had caught him completely off guard. He wasn't being fair to himself or to Melody—his guilt for feeling as he did, for even thinking about moving forward with his life, was a huge obstacle between them and, quite frankly, Melody deserved better.

What awaited him on his return was the life he'd left, the life of a confused, grieving man. He had an empty house, an empty car, an empty life without his wife. All of those possessions, even his job, held no delight for him any more and that's why he wasn't looking forward to the end of the tour.

He shook his head slowly and glanced at Melody, watching her chat animatedly with her registrar. He wasn't that man any more. While the tour had indeed been gruelling, it had helped him find perspective in his grief. He'd been to so many different hospitals, met so many different people from all walks of life. Veronique hadn't wanted this tour to take place in only large teaching hospitals, she'd wanted George to give instruction and hope to surgeons in small hospitals in the developing world where the facilities might not have been state of the art but where the care for patients had been paramount.

He'd done all that. He'd helped people, providing those developing countries not only with new surgical techniques but leaving behind the gift of the device he'd invented, which could cut surgical time in half. He'd done all of those things, provided a lasting legacy for his wife, but what was he supposed to do on his return to Melbourne?

Melody's laughter floated over him and he breathed in a calming breath. That sound, the brightness in her eyes, the way her lips curved—he liked them all. They made him feel alive again, not just a man who was trudging his way through the wilderness. His attraction to Melody may have been instant, it may have knocked him for six, but it had made him *feel* again, and for that he would be grateful for ever.

Still, until he figured out exactly what he wanted to do with his life, he was better off distancing himself. It wasn't fair—to either of them—to trifle with their emotions. He looked at his empty plate, frowning unseeingly at it. He didn't want to stop experiencing these emotions, he liked feeling alive again, but he also knew it was the right thing to do and he prided himself on always being the type of man to do what was right.

'Are you OK?' Melody's soft words cut into his thoughts and he quickly pasted on a smile.

'Yes.'

'You were concentrating so hard on your empty plate that I thought you might be performing a secret male bonding ritual with it.'

George chuckled, feeling instantly better. 'Close but no cigar.'

Melody's mobile phone rang, bringing her back to reality. She quickly connected the call, frowning as she listened to the information. 'I'll be right there,' she replied.

'You don't seem to be able to get through a complete dinner. It's either the beginning or the end,' George jested.

'Anything wrong, Melody?' Andy asked.

'Not really. They want to transfer a patient out of the hospital.'

'Now?' Andy glanced at his watch. 'It's almost midnight.'

'Makes sense,' George replied with a nod. 'They want you to check he's all right to be moved?'

'Yes.'

'Who's the patient?' Andy asked, completely baffled.

'Rudy Carlew,' Melody replied as she stood and collected her bag.

'Rudy Carlew! You operated on Rudy Carlew and you didn't tell me?' Andy asked incredulously.

'Oh, not you too.' Melody laughed. 'Perhaps it's just as well you weren't in Theatre, Andy. We had enough trouble with the theatre nurses drooling over him. I'd better get going. Goodnight,' she said, her gaze encompassing the table in general.

'I'll walk you out,' George offered.

'It's all right, George,' Andy said, quickly gulping his coffee and standing. 'I'll go with her. I'm not going to miss the opportunity of meeting one of my favourite movie stars.'

Melody met George's gaze, a small smile on her lips. He returned the smile and shrugged one shoulder. Again, it appeared they were completely in sync with each other, having an unspoken conversation, but this conversation was one filled with regret at not being able to spend more time together. Even though they knew they shouldn't, what they knew and what was continuing to develop between them were two very different things. 'See you tomorrow, then.'

'Of course.' She took a few steps away, then turned and fixed him with a cheeky stare. 'Uh—will you be there for ward round? I'm just asking—' she hurried on, a teasing glint in her eyes '—so I know whether to start without you.'

George laughed. 'Oh, you're funny. I don't think we're scheduled for ward round but if there's a change, we'll let you know.'

'Just so long as you do it before eight-thirty, otherwise you'll have to join in whenever you get there.' A few of the other people at their table laughed, knowing what had happened that morning.

'We'll do our best,' George responded, and held out his hand to Melody. Deprived of spending a few minutes alone with her, he felt the need to touch her at least. Melody slowly slid her hand into his and held it firmly. Her skin was soft and smooth and George couldn't resist stroking it gently with his thumb.

His gaze met hers and held for a split second. He saw a flash of longing enter her green depths and felt a stirring deep within. Conscious of the people around them, he reluctantly let go of her hand. 'I hope you won't be held up too long at the hospital.'

'You and me both,' she replied, and he was delighted that her tone was a little unsteady, indicating she was as affected by him as he was by her.

'Ready, Melody?' Andy asked, eager to leave.

Melody turned from George, cleared her throat and nodded at her registrar. As they walked out, Andy mumbled, 'I still can't believe you didn't call me to assist you. Rudy Carlew!'

'George was there.'

'George assisted you?'

'Yes. Problem?'

'No.' Andy frowned as they waited for the lift. 'It's just that he's so...*qualified*, and a lower-limb specialist and yet there he was, assisting you.'

'Oh, so I'm not qualified?'

'Come on, Melody. You know what I mean.'

'I do, Andy. George wanted to assist. Think about it. The last time he would have helped out in an emergency situation would have been before he'd started the VOS.'

'I guess a change is as good as a holiday.'

Melody chuckled. 'Something like that.' As they rode the lift down to the ground floor and waited for the valet to retrieve her car, Melody wondered whether her own feelings towards George were because having him around this week was like she was on holiday from her usual schedule. Ordinarily, she'd have clinics, elective surgery, lectures, meetings and the on-call roster to deal with, but this week a lot of things had been postponed to accommodate the VOS schedule. Was that why she was experiencing these emotions towards George? Because it was similar to the sensations of a holiday romance?

Usually, when two people were attracted to each other they would spend an hour here or an hour there, slowly getting to know each other. With George and herself, they'd spent so much time together during the past two days that if she was to proportion out the actual hours, it was as though they'd known each other for at least a month and a half.

The problem was, while she was enjoying the attention, while she was delighted with the way George could make her feel, she knew it couldn't last—but the more time she spent with him, the more she wanted it to. Surely it was good that she was moving forward when it came to her romantic life? That she was willing to accept the attentions of a man and to know that he wasn't out to use or debase her? It was scary, it was mind-blowing and it was...exhilarating.

Once again, Melody had to force thoughts of George from her mind when they arrived at the hospital, especially as it was to find Rudy's manager, Astrid, in a complete tizz. 'Finally! You're here. We need to move him now,' she stormed. 'The fans have all gone home and if we don't do it soon, they'll be back and annoying him again.'

'Isn't that the price of fame?' Melody commented as she started her examination. Andy, who she'd thought might turn into a groupie fan, was the consummate professional.

'You're showing no signs of any complications,' she told Rudy, 'but it's still too early to tell. Where did you say you'd be going?'

'To a hotel,' Astrid answered for him. 'He'll have a private doctor and private nurses to take care of him. So, please, save us all some time and sign him over or he'll just discharge himself.'

Melody clenched her teeth but forced a smile. 'I'll need to talk to the doctor who'll be taking over his treatment,' she said. 'And the nursing staff.'

'Well…we haven't actually employed anyone yet. We just need to get him moved!' Astrid huffed before flipping open her bag and taking out a cigarette. Melody watched her in disbelief.

'Astrid,' Rudy said tiredly, 'put that away. This is a hospital.'

'What? Oh.' Astrid looked at the cigarette in her hand as though she had no idea where it had come from. 'Sorry,' she replied softly, and it was then Melody realised the other woman simply ran on nerves.

'Listen, why don't we sit down and discuss the best course of action for Rudy? He needs to be monitored for the next twenty-four hours at least. I think I might be able to help out in recommending a nurse. As far as a doctor goes, how about Andy…' she gestured to her registrar '…does a house call twice a day? It would only be for the next

few days and after that you'll be fine with weekly or fort-
nightly check-ups.'

Rudy nodded. 'Sounds fair. What do you think, Astrid?'

'As long as it means we can move you now, I don't care.'

'Which hotel will you be staying at?' Melody asked, and
wasn't surprised when he named the hotel where George
was staying. After all, it was Sydney's finest.

'Hey,' Andy remarked, 'we've just come from there.
We had a dinner there this evening. Food was fantastic.'

'Good to hear.' Rudy sighed and closed his eyes. Melody
realised he was exhausted—and rightly so.

'Do you have transport organised?'

'It's all ready to go,' Astrid replied, her impatience returning. 'So can we move him now?'

'Let me arrange the nurse first,' Melody replied, and
headed to the nurses' station to use the phone. She motioned for Andy to follow her. 'I'd like you to monitor him
tonight. Is that all right with you?'

'Sure. Wow! I get to be orthopaedic doctor to Rudy
Carlew.'

Melody smiled. 'Quite a feather in your cap, eh?'

'I'll just head over to the residence where I keep a
change of clothes and meet you back here,' he said, already starting out the door.

Melody sat down and called Switchboard. After obtaining Evelyn's home number, she gave her a call.

'Hi, Evelyn. Sorry to wake you,' Melody said.

'I'm not on call,' Evelyn told her with a yawn. 'I don't
even work there now. Remember?'

'I know, which is why I called. As you were in Theatre
for Rudy Carlew's surgery, and are already familiar with
the case, I was wondering if you wouldn't mind being his
private nurse for the next few weeks.'

'Did I hear you right? No. I must still be asleep and this
is a dream.'

Melody laughed. 'You heard me right, Evelyn. His manager wants him out of the hospital tonight.' Melody gave Evelyn the details of where he was staying. 'We'll be moving him there within the hour.'

'Is Rudy showing any sign of complications?'

'Not yet.'

'Well, you only operated on him a few hours ago so it's too soon to tell,' Evelyn mumbled.

'So will you do it?'

'You'd better believe it,' the nurse replied with a laugh.

'Good. Now, with your nursing agency, you'll need to—'

'I'll take care of it.'

'OK. I'll see you at the hotel.'

Rudy was collected from one of the back entrances to the hospital, after a security sweep by his bodyguards had revealed no fans to be found. Andy rode in the luxurious limousine with Rudy and Astrid, while Melody followed them in her car. At the hotel, Melody met Evelyn by the lifts. 'Oh, good,' Melody said. 'Thanks for doing this at such short notice.'

'Are you kidding?' The nurse giggled. 'This is just the best thing that's ever happened to me. So where is he?'

'Being brought in through the back entrance.' They took the lift up to the fourth floor, which was where a number of fancy suites were located. Astrid had told her the room number but as there were bodyguards standing in the corridor, Melody surmised that they'd beaten Rudy there.

A door marked 'Staff Only' opened and Rudy was brought through in a wheelchair. He was just being taken into the room when a door along the corridor opened. Melody looked around and saw George, dressed in faded denim jeans, a white T-shirt and with damp hair, come through the door.

He stopped when he saw her. 'Melody!'

'George!' Her surprise equalled his. She drank in the sight of him. Dressed in casual clothes and fresh from a shower, the man was even more devastatingly handsome than she'd thought possible. Her heart rate increased and her mouth went dry. The butterflies in her stomach took flight and her knees turned to jelly. Melody leaned against the wall for a moment, feeling slightly dizzy. The man had actually made her swoon!

'Are you all right?' he asked, taking a few steps together her, but one of Rudy's bodyguards intercepted him.

'No. It's all right,' she said quickly, and held up her hand to stop him.

'Ma'am, security has to be kept tight,' the bodyguard replied.

'No. You don't understand. This doctor assisted with Mr Carlew's surgery earlier this evening.'

Astrid came out of the suite. 'What's going on?' she asked, and then spotted George. 'Oh, hi again,' she said. 'It's all right.' Her last comment was directed to the bodyguard. 'Has that other equipment come up yet?'

The 'Staff Only' door opened as she spoke and the equipment, which had been hired from a private hospital, was wheeled through. 'This way,' Astrid instructed. The bodyguard followed her and waited for Melody.

'Uh… I'll be there in a moment. Tell Andy to get things started,' she ordered, and the bodyguard shut the door behind him.

'Doing a little private consulting?' George asked, his tone husky. He didn't move. They simply stood there, staring at each other. Melody's gaze raked over him again and she realised his feet were bare. He looked so…different out of his suit. Relaxed, gorgeous and dangerously sexy!

CHAPTER NINE

HER HEART HAMMERED wildly against her ribs and she was positive he could hear it. Melody tried to swallow but found her throat completely dry. 'I…um…hope the…um…' She trailed off as he took a small step towards her. Her breathing increased and she parted her lips to allow the air to escape more easily, her gaze never once leaving his.

Again, he moved, slowly closing the distance between them. Melody took an involuntary step backwards, only to encounter the wall once more. He was like a lion stalking his prey—slowly, cautiously. She couldn't move even if she wanted to. She was mesmerised by him.

With a few more steps he was standing before her. In her high-heeled shoes, their gazes were almost level. Her gaze flicked to his lips and saw them part.

'Oh,' she gasped as he raised his hands and placed them on the wall on either side of her head. Her breathing was now so utterly out of control there was no hiding just how much this man affected her. She'd been attracted to other men in the past but never had it been this intense.

She looked up into his eyes, noting the mounting desire in him as George slowly leaned closer. His clean, fresh scent only heightened her awareness of him.

'You were saying?' His deep voice washed over her and Melody's eyelids fluttered closed, savouring the moment. She opened them again and looked longingly at his lips.

'Huh?'

'Didn't you want to…ask me something?'

Did she? She had no idea. Her brain failed her, her only conscious thought being that if George didn't kiss her, she'd go insane. The effect he had on her senses was sending them spiralling out of control. Her body was in tune with his as she silently urged him to come even closer.

How much longer was he going to torture them? If she could get her arms to move, she'd reach out and bring his lips to hers. She was paralysed, no, hypnotised and there was nothing she could do about it, such was the effect George had on her.

'Captivating,' he whispered. Never before had he felt like this. It had to be right—but even if it was wrong there was no denying that the only thing he wanted to do right at this very second was to claim Melody's luscious lips in a mind-shattering kiss. A kiss that would satisfy them both—of that he was absolutely sure.

Closer and closer he came until his breath was mixing with hers. Melody closed her eyes, unable to summon the strength to keep them open. She waited—waited impatiently for his mouth to touch hers while still enjoying the sensations he was evoking throughout her body.

The click of a door being opened, together with Andy's voice saying, 'I'll check with Melody,' penetrated the sensual haze with a jolt.

Melody's eyes snapped open, her limbs came to life and she quickly ducked under George's arm, trying to compose herself. Her legs were like jelly and as she took a step away she stumbled.

'Hey, Melody,' Andy said as he spotted her and then quickly held out a steadying hand. 'You all right?'

Not trusting herself to speak, she nodded.

'George?' Andy looked past her and Melody risked a glance over her shoulder. He was casually leaning against the wall, his hands in his jeans pockets.

'Andy.'

'Are you staying on this floor?'

'Yes, a few doors down.' He kept his gaze away from Melody's, although the way she'd looked a few seconds ago would now be burned in his memory for ever. Her face had been turned expectantly up towards his, her lips parted, her eyes closed, her skin tinged with a faint pink glow. Beautiful! 'I hear Rudy Carlew's one of my neighbours.' He forced himself to ease away from the wall.

He was determined to ensure Andy didn't pick up on the sexual tension that existed between Melody and himself. He needed to protect her as best he could and if that meant not looking at her then he wouldn't.

'Yeah, and Melody and I are his doctors,' Andy said excitedly. 'Come and say g'day,' he urged, and knocked on the closed hotel door. It was opened by one of the bodyguards and Andy headed in.

Melody hung back, anxious for a look, a word, something from George to reassure her. Instead, he gave her a wide berth and for the first time since she'd met him he went through the door before her.

She felt hurt. Didn't he realise she needed some reassurance? Had Andy not interrupted them, George would have kissed her and there was no way she would have fought him. She'd wanted it just as desperately as he had.

Feeling suddenly cold and bereft, Melody rubbed her arms as the first spark of anger ignited deep within. Why was it she felt as though she'd done something wrong when she knew she hadn't? She surmised it was because both Ian and Emir, whenever things had gone wrong or hadn't gone the way they'd wanted, had always shunned her, shutting her out, making her feel as though everything had been her fault.

Didn't George want her? Was he just playing with her? She shook her head, not wanting to believe it. Her old neuroses were rising to the surface. Emir had told her he hadn't wanted children but his decision to follow his pregnant mistress to Germany had helped Melody realise the truth—namely that Emir hadn't wanted to have children *with her.* He hadn't wanted to marry *her.* Now George was acting the same. Now that he had her dangling from his hook, he wasn't interested in more. Was that the case? Was he only interested in the chase?

She followed him into Rudy's room. How dared he pretend nothing had almost happened between them? Why hadn't he given her a little smile or a yearning look to let her know that they were still in sync, that they could still have these unspoken conversations even when other people were around?

She hated feeling like this, having her thoughts all jumbled when she needed to have clear, calm and collected thoughts. More to the point, why was she allowing him to have such power over her, to affect her in such a way? Her anger grew and it encompassed herself as well as George.

Perhaps she should thank Andy for interrupting them. Perhaps she should consider this a lucky escape. After all, if they had kissed, then she would have had more physical sensations to fight. Perhaps she was better off.

'Would that be right, Melody?' Andy was asking her, and she realised that everyone in the room was looking at her expectantly—except George.

'Uh—well—um…' she stumbled, not at all sure what Andy had asked.

'I think you're spot on, Andy,' George answered. 'Good work.'

'Ah—absolutely,' Melody responded, finally finding her voice. Her hostility towards George diminished a bit as she acknowledged that he'd just rescued her. She needed to get out of there, to sort out her emotions before she made a fool of herself. 'If that's all you need…' she glanced at Rudy and then at Andy, her gaze eluding George's '… I think I'll head home. It's been a very hectic day and tomorrow promises to be no less so. Call me if you need me,' she told Andy as she turned and headed to the door, the burgundy dress swishing around her ankles.

'I'd better be going too,' George announced to the room.

'Aw—come on,' Astrid purred, and Melody watched as the other woman crossed to George's side and linked her arm through his. 'Surely you don't have to go just yet? Now that we've got Rudy settled, we can all relax and have some fun.'

'Ugh,' Melody groaned softly, and continued to the door one of the bodyguards held open for her. 'Relax and have some fun,' she mimicked softly as she stormed over to the lifts. 'That man doesn't know his own charm and probably has every woman he meets falling in love with him.' She assaulted the down button, pressing it repeatedly.

'Mumbling to yourself?' George asked from behind her, and although Melody's body shivered in excitement at the sound of his voice, she didn't turn around. Instead, she pressed the down button again.

'I'll walk you out.'

'There's no need,' she replied between clenched teeth.

George watched as she pressed the button again, muttering something about slow hotel lifts. He frowned, unsure why she was so angry. 'It's no trouble,' he told her.

Melody spun to glare at him. 'I don't care if it's an imposition to you or not, the fact is that I don't want you to walk me out. I'm a big girl, George, and I'm more than capable of riding in the lift, walking to the valet desk and waiting for my car.' She pressed the button. 'That's if this lift ever gets here.'

'Why are you angry with me again?' He spread his arms wide.

'Oh, this is all *my* fault?' Her temper was at boiling point. She was cross with him, cross with herself and cross with the lift. She glanced around for an exit sign and stormed over to the door marked 'Stairs'.

'Melody!' George charged after her, completely baffled as to why she was upset. The concrete stairs were cold beneath his feet but that was the least of his worries. 'Talk to me,' he demanded, his voice echoing. The clip-clop of Melody's shoes reverberated around the stairwell and he was pleased to note she was holding onto the railing. The last thing she needed was a twisted ankle.

'There's nothing to say.' She rounded the bend and started on the next flight. She was grateful that Rudy's suite hadn't been on the twentieth floor but given the way she was feeling she wouldn't have cared how many flights of stairs she had to walk down. All she wanted was to get out of the hotel and away from George.

'Nothing to say? You're being stubborn and irrational.'

Melody stopped and whirled around to look up at him. He stopped too. 'Stubborn? Irrational?'

'Yes.' There were only two steps between them and George slowly moved down one, hoping she wouldn't move. It didn't work.

She whirled around again and started clopping her way down the noisy stairwell. 'So what if I am being irrational? I've got good reason.'

'Then tell me what it is so I can apologise.'

'It's the fact that you don't know you've done anything wrong that's made me angry.' That and her own uncontrollable reaction to him. She had to become stronger. She had to fight the attraction between them with every ounce of her strength.

'Wanting to kiss you was wrong?'

'Oh, you know it was,' she growled. 'And then you want to pretend it didn't happen.'

'But it *didn't* happen,' he returned.

'Not the kiss, that's not what I'm talking about.'

'Then what are you talking about? I'm completely perplexed about why I'm suddenly in the doghouse when, as far as I'm concerned, I've done nothing wrong.'

'Isn't that always the way with you men?' She threw over her shoulder as she continued her descent. 'And then there's Astrid and goodness knows how many other women throwing themselves at you, day and night.'

'That's hardly my fault—and I'm not with Astrid, I'm with you.'

'Because you're hoping to pick up where we left off?' she queried. 'You didn't get to kiss me, so now you'll chase after me in the hope that you'll get what you want in the end?' She clicked her tongue disapprovingly. 'You men really are all the same.'

'You keep saying that,' George argued back. 'Are you really comparing me to the dead-heads you've dated in the past?'

'Dead-heads? They were both qualified doctors and you don't even know them.'

'They broke your heart. That means they were not only stupid but idiotic, and I don't care how many university degrees they held. A qualification doesn't give you licence to treat people badly.' His words were harsh and filled with annoyance. Was he annoyed at her or at the dead-heads she'd dated?

'At any rate, it's none of your business.' She rounded the corner for the final flight of stairs.

'It *is* my business if you're going to tar me with the same brush as them.'

'How can I? I hardly know you, George. You tell me you're attracted to me, that no other woman has made you feel this way since—' She stopped and sighed, not wanting to have a discussion about his wife because she really only knew what George had told her and therefore had no authority to speak about it.

'My wife,' he finished for her. 'Yes, that's true.'

'That's what you *tell* me. You've been travelling for so long, you're bound to get—well—lonely and…'

'So you just think I try and kiss any woman who shows an interest in me, eh?'

'How do I know? You might.' The last thing Melody wanted to think about now was George kissing other women. Jealousy reared its ugly head.

'Even though we've spent such a short time together, Melody, I thought the answer to that question might have been obvious. For all I know, you might be the type of woman who gives in to every guy who makes a pass at you.'

'What?' She stopped walking long enough to turn and glare at him. 'How dare you?'

'Ah, so you don't like either. It's all right for you to accuse me of awful behaviour but not vice-versa.' He came to stand beside her on the step, both of them staring at each other, their emotions rioting. Melody was still annoyed with him for withdrawing from her the way he had, for pretending that almost-kiss hadn't happened and that she—she— He'd made her feel unworthy but she wasn't sure how to voice such a thing given she really had no idea where or if this attraction between them was going anywhere.

Melody looked down at the stairs, trying to control her emotions and her thoughts. Finally, she raised her head to look into his eyes, eyes that had the ability to make her forget all rational thought. 'Look, all I was saying is that you're a very handsome man and I'm sure you've met plenty of women during the VOS who would have been more than willing to indulge in a brief affair while you were in town.'

'And what if there were?'

Melody's eyes widened in surprise. Was he admitting to it? Was he a womaniser? 'Were there?' she asked quietly, trying hard to control her disappointment.

'Yes.'

She felt as though he'd hit her. Her mouth opened in disbelief. She'd been hoping against hope that he wasn't that way and now he was admitting as much. Turning, she started walking down the stairs again, thankful she was almost at the lobby. George, however, was clearly fed up with everything and took the stairs two at a time, passing her and barring her way just before she reached the door that led to the lobby.

'Yes, there have been women who've made passes at me during the VOS, but I didn't take any of them up on their offers. Melody, I've been working through a lot of emotions during this tour and the last thing I needed was… entanglements.' He held out his hand to her. 'Until you.' His tone was soft and endearing, urging her to trust him.

She looked at his hand but didn't take it. He dropped it back to his side and nodded. 'You're the first woman I've wanted to kiss since Veronique. Is it so wrong that I'd follow through on that instinct?'

'Perhaps not, but it was what you did afterwards.'

'What? Protecting you against gossip? Trying not to let Andy see that he'd almost caught us together?' His words were earnest. 'I don't want to leave you with more to deal with after I leave.'

Melody closed her eyes. He'd been trying to protect her? Was that just a line? An excuse for his behaviour? She'd heard so many excuses from Ian and Emir in the past that it was difficult to know whether George was speaking the truth. Opening her eyes, she sidestepped him and stalked through the door into the lobby.

'And as far as the almost-kiss goes,' he continued as he went after her, 'you were quite willing for it to happen, too.'

Melody stopped and turned to face him, glad that, except for the bare minimum of staff, the lobby was deserted. 'I am not having this discussion with you here.'

'Then come back up to my room and we'll discuss it there.'

'Ha. Come back to your room? That should be the last thing I do.'

'Why?'

Melody opened her mouth to speak but couldn't. She

wanted to tell him that if she went up to his room, there was no way she'd be able to resist him. He would kiss her and she would willingly let him. She knew it was because she wanted it, more than she wanted anything else right now, but she'd also given in to her wants before and it had ended in heartbreak.

'I'll tell you why,' he continued. 'You don't want to come back to my room because you can't trust yourself.' He lowered his voice and took a step closer. As he did so, he stubbed his toe on a nearby table and grunted in pain.

Melody reached out and steadied the vase of flowers on the table before glancing down at his foot. He'd flexed his ankle to hold the toes upwards and was hobbling towards a chair. She looked into his eyes and saw the pain there.

'Let me look at it,' she said, and reached for his foot.

'No. It's fine. I can take care of it.'

'Stop being such a martyr and let me look at it.' Melody grabbed his heel and lifted it up.

'Is everything all right?' one of the staff asked.

'It's fine.' George glared at Melody as she tweaked his sore toe.

'Sorry.' She continued checking the range of motion. 'Not broken,' she announced, and turned to face the staff member. 'He'll be fine,' she said. 'My prescription is two paracetamol and bed rest. Perhaps you might help Professor Wilmont to the lift so he can get back up to his room?' Melody smiled sweetly, enjoying George's disadvantage.

'I'm fine,' he repeated, and stood to prove it.

'Well, if that's all, I'll be on my way.' Melody handed the staff member her valet ticket and after a brief nod he left them alone again. 'No charge for the examination,' she told George.

'How generous of you.' He frowned and she realised that she'd better not try to push him any further as his mood had changed drastically. Previously, he'd been willing to reason, to discuss things calmly. Now he wasn't in such a good mood and she didn't blame him—stubbed toes were painful.

Melody decided to take pity on him. 'Go and rest. I'll see you tomorrow,' she said, and turned away from him. It was either that or throw herself into his arms. He looked so gorgeous, standing there in his faded denims, his brown eyes telling of his exhaustion. It had been hard to resist but with every step she took away from him, she grew more proud of her success.

'Melody,' he called softly, and she turned around, gazing at him expectantly.

'Thanks.'

'For what?'

'For talking to me.'

Was he trying to make her feel guilty? Emir had often used that tactic and she'd fallen for it every time. His next words, however, made her rethink.

'I know it wasn't easy for you and I appreciate it.' His gaze bored into hers and she felt that familiar stirring sensation in her stomach. 'Drive carefully.' With that, he turned and hobbled over to the lift. Melody watched him, torn between amusement at the sight he made and the urge to assist him.

'Your car is here, ma'am.'

Melody forced herself to look away and walked out of the hotel. George pressed the button for the lift and glanced her way. She was magnificent, and she had become far too important to him, far too quickly.

The lift bell chimed and George hobbled in, recalling the way he'd felt as she'd cradled his foot in her hand. As she'd been angry with him, he'd half expected her to be rough with her examination but, instead, she'd been extremely gentle. Her skin had been soft against his and although she'd touched him in a professional, medical way, George hadn't been able to stop the stirring of excitement that had shot through him.

At the fourth floor, he walked to his door and reached into his back pocket for the key card. Once inside, he opened the curtains and turned off the lights before settling back on the bed, propping his foot up on a few pillows.

He'd come so close to kissing her—so agonisingly close. Ever since they'd met, George had wanted to sample her mouth and the longer he waited, the more urgent the desire grew.

He knew the score. He knew she didn't want to get hurt and he had no desire to hurt her. He raked an unsteady hand though his hair and groaned in confusion. What about Veronique? Would she mind if he kissed another woman? The feelings of betrayal hit him forcefully but it still didn't stop him from making a decision. He'd be leaving at the end of the week and, regardless of the war taking place inside him, he knew one thing for sure.

Despite everything—he needed to kiss Melody.

CHAPTER TEN

MELODY DIDN'T SLEEP at all well that night and when she did manage to drift off sometime before dawn, she dreamt she was anxiously trying to glue a vase back together. The pieces were tiny and the tears she was crying kept blurring her vision. She stood and looked down at the mess and only then did she realise that the vase was heart-shaped.

The realisation only increased the urgency as she was expecting a new delivery of flowers at any minute. Working frantically, Melody managed to piece the heart-shaped vase back together. The doorbell rang and she hurried to open it. There stood George, holding a bunch of roses. Melody stared aghast at the vase. She couldn't accept the flowers from George because the vase was still drying.

She wanted the flowers but where was she going to put them? Anxiousness and fear gripped Melody's heart as George held the flowers out to her. What was she going to do?

She sat bolt upright in bed, her heart pounding fiercely against her ribs. 'Just a dream,' she whispered to herself. She lay back and sighed, breathing deeply. She glanced at the clock and realised it was one minute before her alarm was due to go off. 'So much for a good night's sleep,' she muttered, and clambered out of bed.

She glanced at herself in the mirror. She looked horrible. 'Perhaps a little make-up might be in order today.' Melody finished getting dressed, deciding that she wouldn't chance breakfast as her stomach didn't feel settled.

She arrived at the hospital and went straight to the ward. All through the round, she kept anxiously glancing at the door in case George decided to join them again. He didn't. Feeling a bit flat, she returned to her office, hoping to catch up on paperwork before her theatre list began in half an hour.

Sitting at her desk, it wasn't long before further thoughts of George intruded and, instead of fighting them, she gave in. She was exhausted from fighting her emotions, as well as lack of sleep. She thought about her dream, reflecting on the symbolism of the heart-shaped vase. It was true that Emir had broken her heart but she'd managed to mend it.

With George, her feelings for him were so out of proportion in comparison to what she'd previously felt. She'd been committed to marrying Emir, to spending the rest of her life with him. He'd been a charmer, just like George. He'd been a gentleman, just like George. He'd been a dashingly handsome man, just like George. He'd wooed her, made her feel special, made her feel as though she was valued.

Well, George hadn't wooed her exactly, but he did make her feel special. Melody realised the biggest difference between George and Emir was that George appreciated her intelligence, that he treated her as though she had a brain to talk things out, to be open and honest. Right from the start George had been upfront about the attraction between them, and although she wasn't used to a man treating her in such a caring and thoughtful way, it was very refreshing. Refreshing and scary because it only endeared him to her more. She wanted to spend time with him, talk to him, laugh with him, press her mouth to his and hold him close.

Somehow, in such a short time, George had managed to break down the barriers she'd so carefully erected. Back when she'd split with Emir, she'd told herself she preferred loneliness rather than being used, but loneliness wasn't the greatest thing in the world, not when she went home to an empty apartment after long and exhausting shifts at the hospital.

Whether this thing between them was something temporary or permanent, didn't she owe it to herself to find out? What if George *was* the one for her, the one she would spend the rest of her life with, and she'd let him go? What if—?

A knock at her office door startled her out of her deep reverie and she jumped in her chair, clutching her hand to her chest as Rick sauntered into the room.

'Finished with that file yet?'

'Huh? Oh, sorry.' She looked down at the open file and realised that she hadn't started. So much for getting through her paperwork. 'Not yet.'

'Everything all right?' he asked.

'Yes.'

'Sure? You seem to be…preoccupied.'

She shrugged and looked down, not wanting him to see the tell-tale blush she could feel creeping into her cheeks. 'It's been a busy few days,' she rationalised.

'It certainly has. Today, thankfully, isn't going to be as hectic.' Rick went over her schedule, which included her operating list that morning and time to work on her research project in the afternoon. 'Then there's a dinner this evening.'

Melody groaned. 'Do I have to go?' It wasn't that she didn't want to see George, she did, but she didn't want to see him surrounded by a room full of other people. She wanted to spend time with him one on one, to really talk, to really start to get to know the man better than she did.

'Yes. You do,' Rick told her. 'And now you need to go to Theatre. Starting your list late will not make anyone happy.'

Melody stood. 'What would I do without you, Rick?'

'Fall flat on your face and fail,' he answered with a cheeky grin.

Chuckling, Melody left her office and headed to Elective Theatres. Everything progressed smoothly and she de-gowned just after midday, pleased with what she could accomplish when she pushed thoughts of George aside.

With determination in her step, she headed to the medical research building and walked into her lab. She chatted with the technician who was a collaborator on her research project and spent a good two hours working. Once that was done she headed back to her office determined to tackle her paperwork. So far she'd managed to have a very productive day and she was positive it was because she'd hardly thought about George at all.

Back at her office, she managed a steady half-hour of work before being called to the ED to consult on a case with Dr Okanadu. She was in the doctors' tea room, eating an exceptionally late lunch, studying the X-rays on the computer screen, when the door opened and closed. She didn't break focus to see who had walked in.

'Interesting case?'

A flood of excitement washed over her at the sound of George's voice. She looked up in surprise, right into his deep brown eyes, eyes that were gazing at her with repressed desire. She breathed in and swallowed at the same time, choking on the last mouthful of her sandwich. She coughed violently and George patted her on the back.

'Take it easy,' he said, quickly fetching a glass of water.

'I'm fine,' she whispered, but then coughed again, proving herself wrong.

'You seem to be forever choking,' he jested.

'Only when you're around,' she mumbled as she took a sip. She cleared her throat. 'What brings you to the hospital?' His spicy scent entwined itself around her and she fought hard to resist it.

'Aren't I allowed to call in without an invitation?' He smiled as he leant against the edge of the table. His firm thigh was so close to her arm that she could feel the heat radiating from him. Her breath caught in her throat and her mouth went dry.

Melody took another sip of water. 'No, it's just that… I thought you were lecturing.'

'I was.' He glanced at the computer screen and winced. 'Ouch.' He frowned at the image. 'What on earth happened to your patient?'

'She caught her hand in a conveyor belt. I'll be using this case for my research.' Melody glanced at the clock. 'I want to get to Theatre soon to make a start on it.' Why was she so aware of him? She closed the file on the computer and went to turn the monitor off but accidentally brushed his leg with the back of her hand. An explosion, similar to fireworks, burst through her, and her eyelids fluttered closed for a brief second. When she glanced at him, it was to discover he was gazing down at her with burning desire.

George fought hard for control but it wasn't easy. She set him on fire. With the mildest touch, with the momentary flutter of her eyes, with the perfume that was driving him insane. She set him on fire and he was sick of dousing the flames.

He fought for something to say. 'Er…how many reconstructions have you done like this one?' He couldn't help the huskiness that accompanied his words and as Melody looked away, he feasted his eyes on the slender, smooth skin of her neck. Her hair was clipped back at her nape and he remembered how incredible it had looked flowing freely around her face last night.

'Um…quite a few.' She shifted her chair slightly, trying to put a bit of distance between them without appearing rude.

'Are you operating in the theatre with the viewing gallery?'

'No.'

'Pity.'

'Why?'

'This type of operation should be recorded for future reference.'

'There are already a few in the hospital's library,' she told him as she gathered her notes, and he noticed her hands weren't quite steady.

'Ones you've done?' He could see she was getting ready to take flight and he wanted to stop her. If he edged a little to the side and bent his head, he was positive he'd be able to capture her sweet lips in his. Lips he ached to taste.

'Yes.'

'I'm impressed.'

'Really?' She looked up at him from where she sat, warmed by his praise. Here was a man who had worked with some of the finest surgeons in the world, and he was impressed because some of her operations had been recorded?

'Yes.' He gazed into her eyes and leaned closer. 'I know only the most impressive surgery is recorded.' Unable to resist touching her any longer, he reached out and tenderly ran his fingers down her cheek, bringing them to rest beneath her chin. 'Melody.' As he breathed her name, he lifted her chin slightly, angling her head towards his.

Melody gazed at him, her heart pounding wildly against her ribs. He was going to kiss her. This time, for sure, he was going to kiss her. She watched from beneath her lashes as his head slowly drew closer. She shouldn't be doing this. She had an operation to concentrate on.

'George... I—' She didn't manage to finish her sentence as his mouth finally made contact with hers, and she gasped with anticipatory delight. George groaned as she leaned closer to him. Her lips were soft and pliable, just as he'd known they would be.

Melody sighed and opened her mouth beneath his subtle urging, elated to finally give in to her feelings. He tasted like chocolate and coffee—both sweet and addictive.

Without breaking contact, his hands cupped her face, urging her closer, and she edged from her chair, reaching out for him as she moved to stand in front of him. She was amazed to find her usually wobbly legs were willing to support her.

He shifted to accommodate her, his hands sliding around her back as he deepened the kiss. Never in his wildest dreams had he imagined torture could be so agonisingly delightful. She simply melted into his embrace as though they'd been made for each other. The realisation only increased the overpowering emotions swamping him.

Fireworks like she'd never felt before exploded one after the other throughout her body, each new burst sending her senses spiralling out of control. This was impossible. Never before had she been so overwhelmed by a kiss. Then again, this wasn't any ordinary kiss. The spark that flowed freely between them now, had been repressed for two and a half full days, building and simmering within, only to be unleashed with such intensity.

Her hands were pressed against his chest and she could feel the contours of his firm, muscled torso beneath his cotton shirt. Delighted at being able to touch him at last, she slid her hands up his chest, entwining them about his neck, her fingers plunging into his rich, dark hair. A low guttural sound, primitive, came from him and she revelled in her power.

His hands slid ever so slowly down her sides, his fingers splayed, moulding her ribs. His thumbs lightly brushed the underside of her breasts and she gasped in shock as yet another wave of pleasure coursed through her.

Her excitement was mounting with every passing second and she was having difficulty breathing. What did she care about oxygen when she had George? With a satisfied moan, Melody pulled her mouth from his, dragging air into her lungs, pleased to note that his breathing was just as erratic as hers.

He pressed kisses to her cheek, working his way towards her ear, and she tipped her head to the side, allowing him access. A thousand goose-bumps cascaded over her body, increasing her light-headedness. He was a drug and the more she had of him, the more she knew she'd become addicted.

He brought his hand up and brushed her neck, gently urging her collar aside to make room for his hungry lips. She had the smoothest skin and the most luscious lips. Now that he'd kissed her, the realisation of how incredible they were together only made him want her even more.

His mouth met hers again, their lips mingling together like old friends. Although he wanted nothing more than to deepen the kiss, heightening the intensity, George could feel her starting to withdraw.

He pressed his lips to hers one last time before allowing her to rest her head on his chest, their breathing slowly returning to normal. His arms embraced her, holding her tightly, never wanting to let her go.

As she stood there, listening to his heart gradually return to a steady rhythm, Melody started to feel uncomfortable and awkward. What would happen now? George had kissed her and it had been…mind-blowing. Her frazzled thoughts acknowledged that she would never be the same again. The kisses, the passion, the desire—everything had changed. *Never* had she experienced anything like the onslaught of emotions or the intensity of feeling that had just taken place.

His hands rubbed gently up and down her back. She knew it was supposed to relax her but all it did was increase her anxiety. Why had she let George kiss her? She was due in Theatre. He would leave at the end of the week. He was still in love with the memory of his wife. She eased from his hold and took three giant steps backwards.

Helplessness and confusion were running rampant

through her mind and along with it came fatigue. She didn't have the energy for a post-mortem on what had just happened and she hoped George realised that. She tucked a stray curl behind her ear and shook her head.

'We shouldn't have done that.' Her words were a whisper.

'Why not?'

'Well, for starters, someone could have walked in and caught us.' She pointed to the door.

'They didn't.'

'I'm due in Theatre soon. I should be concentrating. Hand reconstruction isn't the same as a knee arthroscopy, you know.' She turned and walked over to the kitchen bench, bracing her hands on the edge.

'I know the difference,' he replied, and she heard him walk towards her. She was so instinctively aware of him it frightened her. George rubbed his hands up and down her arms, making her resent her outburst. 'I apologise for the timing. You're right. You should be concentrating.'

He dropped his hands, although he didn't move back. Melody felt slightly bereft but drew warmth from the nearness of his body.

'We do, however,' he continued, 'need to talk.'

'No, we don't.' She turned to look at him, determination running through her body. 'We don't need to discuss or dissect what just happened, George. It happened. Let's just leave it at that. Now, if you'll excuse me, I need to get my thoughts in order regarding this operation.' With that, she sidestepped him and walked to the table.

She collected her notes, conscious of his gaze on her. When she reached the door, she congratulated herself on not giving in to the urge to throw herself back into his arms. Just before she opened the door, he spoke.

'We do need to talk, Melody, and we will.'

She glanced over her shoulder, to see brown eyes that

had not too long ago been filled with desire were now filled with determination. Not trusting herself to say anything, she continued out the door, heading to the emergency theatres, determined to push all thoughts of George Wilmont aside and do her job.

CHAPTER ELEVEN

GEORGE STOOD IN the tea room for a good ten minutes after she'd walked out. His thoughts were completely jumbled and he was having a difficult time making head or tail of them. He'd kissed Melody—he'd kissed another woman!

Guilt swamped him and he closed his eyes. The guilt wasn't only because he felt as though he was cheating on his wife, but the fact that he'd actively pursued Melody, desperate to taste the sweetness of her mouth. He'd *wanted* to kiss her and the guilt from that alone was enough to keep him company for a very long time. What kind of man did that make him? He'd always thought himself honourable, trusting and sincere.

Well, he'd been sincere about kissing Melody. He'd been trusting that his feelings were reciprocated. But honourable? His thoughts had hardly been honourable as he'd held her against him, pressing his mouth to hers, wanting her as close as possible.

What had he been thinking? He had responsibilities. He had a job to do. His behaviour was far from professional yet at the same time it was becoming increasingly difficult to control his desire where Melody was concerned.

She was interfering with his work, his concentration, and it wouldn't do. Right at this moment he was supposed to be working with his staff but he'd needed to see her, needed to touch her, needed to kiss her.

He opened his eyes and paced the room, forcing his thoughts into order. He'd kissed a woman who wasn't Veronique. His wife had died only eighteen months ago and here he was yearning for someone else. He was sure that if their positions had been reversed, Veronique wouldn't have forgotten him so quickly and the knowledge stabbed at his heart.

George grimaced, pushing his fingers roughly through his hair and clenching his jaw. Never before had he allowed any woman to come between him and his work. He'd always separated them into neat little sections. He'd always prided himself on being one hundred percent focused where work was concerned but now he appeared to have no control whatsoever.

He had the responsibilities of the visiting orthopaedic surgeon Fellowship to uphold. He had responsibilities to his staff. He had lectures to write, operations to perform and scheduled deadlines to meet. Even when the tour finished in early December, he was due back at his hospital in Melbourne. They were waiting for him. He had obligations there as well.

Yet one look at Melody and everything had gone! Gone! He shoved his hands in his pockets, thoroughly disgusted with himself and his behaviour. How could a woman make him lose control—over everything? Everything he'd prided himself on being. Reliable, responsible, respectable.

'Ha!' he snorted in self-disgust. He hadn't even treated Melody with respect. She'd been studying and trying to focus on an extremely difficult procedure and he hadn't cared. Hadn't given her the same consideration he was sure she would have given him had the situations been reversed.

He stopped pacing, his jaw clenched tightly. He shouldn't have kissed her. Shouldn't have—but he had. At least he was man enough to accept his actions and take responsibility for them.

George dragged a deep breath into his lungs, the faint

traces of her perfume lingering in the air around him. The awareness between them had been almost unbearable yet now—now both knew how incredible they were together. Kissing Melody hadn't solved anything. It had only increased his desire, his yearning, his curiosity—and that made everything worse!

Melody was tired of concentrating. She'd had three long and meticulous hours in Theatre but at last the first stage of her patient's hand reconstruction was completed. Now they needed to wait and see what happened before she could attempt the next stage.

Wearily, she de-gowned and shuffled to the tea room to write up the notes. Once she'd finished, she sipped her coffee and put her feet up on the seat. Closing her eyes, she sighed, glad the day was coming to an end. 'Just the dinner to get through.'

She'd hoped to get out of it altogether but she knew that wasn't professional. 'I hate being Acting Director,' she mumbled out loud as she quickly finished her coffee.

Melody had hoped to be able to go home, enjoy a relaxing bubble bath, but now she would just have to make do with a quick shower before getting dressed and heading to the hotel for yet another event. She was looking forward to George's talk this evening. She was still constantly amazed that with so many dinners and lectures, he still managed to keep every talk fresh and interesting.

'George,' she sighed, as she drove home and headed into her apartment. If she didn't at least make an appearance tonight, she had the strange feeling he'd probably ring to make sure she was all right. She smiled at the thought. That was nice. Attentive and thoughtful. Apart from kissing her right before she'd had to perform an intricate surgical procedure, he'd always been attentive and thoughtful. Then again, while he'd been kissing her, he'd most definitely been attentive and thoughtful.

She couldn't help but smile and brush a hand across her lips as she remembered just how attentive he'd been. As she finished getting dressed, tonight choosing to wear a white embroidered bustier and a straight, black, silk skirt that came to her ankles, she couldn't help but wonder what George might think of her outfit, especially the split at the back of the skirt, which was not only sexy but practical as it enabled her to walk without shuffling along. She secured her hair up in a high ponytail, letting her curls do their thing. Slipping her stockinged feet into black shoes then picking up her clutch purse, she was finally ready to go.

She couldn't quell her excitement at seeing George again. She was eager to see his reaction to her outfit. To glimpse that smouldering desire in the brown depths of his eyes. To feel her heartbeat increase when he looked at her. To hope for another forbidden kiss.

She drove with care to the function centre and walked through the door at eight o'clock, only half an hour late. She casually walked over to the corner of the room and, holding her breath, searched for George.

'From the back, you look ravishing,' a deep voice said from directly behind her. His breath fanned down her bare neck and Melody couldn't help the shiver of delight that raced through her. 'I don't know if I'm game enough for you to turn around,' he whispered. 'You have the sexiest legs I've ever seen.'

Melody was thankful the room was now swarming with people as waiters brought out trays of food. She had no idea what to say to George. Her mind had gone blank the instant he'd spoken and all she'd been aware of had been the richness of his voice and the emotions he'd stirred up in her.

'Are you purposely trying to drive me insane?' he asked as she slowly turned to face him.

'And if I am?' she challenged, a twinkle of delight in her eyes.

George's smile increased. 'Are you flirting with me, Dr Janeway?'

Melody laughed, amazed at how a few seconds in his company increased her excitement. 'Feels a lot like it, from what I can recall.'

'You are…' he paused, his gaze filled with desire as he looked down into her eyes '…irresistible.'

'I think I'm moving up in the world,' Melody replied, and at George's frown she continued, 'Well, last night you said I was beautiful. The night before you said I was stunning. Tonight it's irresistible.'

He nodded, a slight smile playing on his lips. 'That's because I remember how good you felt in my arms. I'd give anything right now to take you out of here so we can be—' He stopped. 'Ah—yes—hello again, Mr Okanadu.' George quickly changed his tone as he reached over and shook hands with Melody's colleague.

'How did you get on with the surgery, Melody?' Mr Okanadu asked.

George instantly felt like a heel. He'd been so busy admiring Melody that he'd completely forgotten she'd spent the better part of the afternoon performing a difficult piece of surgery. He listened to her reply, glad to hear the patient was doing well.

Moments later, Carmel came over and instructed George it was time for his speech and that they should all return to their tables. George gave his speech, once again adjusting the material to make it fresh and informative. Melody admired him and his professionalism. She also noted that when he sat back down again he moved his chair slightly closer to hers.

In fact, by the time they'd finished their main meal she could feel the warmth emanating from George's leg so close to her own. She tried hard to focus on what Mr Okanadu was saying, nodding and smiling politely, all the while unbearably conscious of George. She could hear her heart thumping wildly against her ribs, could feel the pinpricks of excitement coursing down her spine, could feel her body crying out for his touch. Her reaction was becoming too intrusive and she sternly told herself to stop it.

'Don't you agree?' Mr Okanadu was saying, and Melody hadn't the faintest idea of what he'd been talking about. Once more, she'd been too caught up in thoughts of George that her mind seemed unable to function.

She frowned thoughtfully and said, 'Hmm,' as well as nodding slightly.

'Excuse me,' George said, and Melody quickly turned to give him her attention. He saw an unmistakable hint of passion reflected in her green eyes and for a moment he lost his train of thought. His gut twisted with delight and despair. Things were starting to get way out of hand. 'Ahh…' He frowned and nearly groaned in frustration as her lips parted, her breathing marginally audible. He swallowed, watching as her gaze flicked down to his mouth before returning to his eyes.

It was then his sluggish brain registered that she was waiting for him to speak. Although the looks they'd exchanged seemed to have happened in slow motion, George knew it had only been a few seconds. At least, he hoped it had. Melody had the ability to make him forget all rational thought and in some ways he resented it. No other woman had affected him that way before—not even Veronique.

He cleared his throat. 'Er…you said there were several recordings in the hospital library of other surgeries you've performed, correct?'

'Ye—' Her voice broke and she realised her mouth was dry. She coughed and George immediately held out her water glass. 'Thank you.' She took a quick sip and nodded her head as she replaced her glass. 'Yes.'

'How long ago did you do them?'

She thought for a moment, realising that the person on the other side of George was also listening intently to their conversation. Oh, she hoped and prayed that no one could read the emotions in her eyes when she looked at the visiting surgeon! 'One was in February this year and the other was July. In both cases we've also recorded the follow-up visits, thereby keeping a complete record of any of the after-effects from the surgery.'

'And you're planning to use this case for your research project?'

'This patient will be included, along with the other patients from February and July.'

'Good.' He cleared his throat. 'Uh—I have an evening off tomorrow and I'd be interested in viewing those recordings. Do you think the hospital library will let me borrow them?'

Melody felt the beginning of a smile twitching at her lips. 'Oh, I'm sure they would.'

George watched her lips, noticing she was trying to suppress a smile. He glanced over his shoulder to see that the person next to him was now talking to someone else. He returned his attention to Melody. 'What?' Even as he asked the question, he could feel the tug of his own lips turning upwards. Her eyes were alive with amusement and his gut twisted again at the sight.

'Oh, nothing,' she replied coyly.

'Come on,' he coaxed, his tone dropping to a more intimate level. He was enjoying teasing her a little.

'I'm just in awe of the glamorous life you lead.'

'Meaning?'

'Meaning that on your only night off in Sydney you're choosing to sit in a hotel room and watch a recording on hand reconstruction.' She paused, smothering the laugh. 'What a party animal.'

George's smile increased. 'Who said I was going to be sitting in a hotel room?'

'Oh, you mean you're going to watch it somewhere at the hospital? You certainly know how to have a good time.'

'No. Actually…' he leaned in a little closer '… I was planning to watch it at your place.' As he eased back, George took great delight in watching her amusement slip away, to be replaced by a startled look as the full impact of his words registered.

He shifted slightly and leaned his arm on the back of his chair. As he did so, his serviette slid to the floor. Bending down to retrieve it, he decided to add fuel to the fire and gently brushed a finger on an exposed part of her calf.

The brief contact made Melody jump, her knee hitting the base of the table, jostling the silver- and glassware on top. Conversations stopped. People looked at her. She could feel herself beginning to blush with embarrassment and smiled quickly.

'Sorry. Patellar reflex,' she explained. Everyone returned to what they'd been doing while Melody glanced down at her fingers, which were clenched tightly around her clutch purse. She needed to get control. She needed to get out of there.

Putting her serviette onto the table, she smiled politely at those around her as she stood. 'Excuse me.' With that, she forced herself not to rush but to walk calmly and steadily away from the table. She could feel George's gaze watching her but she forced herself not to care. How could he have put her in such a situation? What had possessed him to touch her in such an intimate manner?

Her head started to hurt. It had been a long day and when she entered the restroom for a moment of peace and quiet, Melody leaned her hands on the bench top and closed her eyes. She was fatigued, and on top of that she was desperately fighting her mounting attraction to George.

After a few minutes she felt more in control and better able to cope with the rest of the evening. Taking a deep breath, she headed back but as she drew closer to the dining room she detoured to the right and through the French doors that led to the balcony.

'How's that patellar reflex?'

There was no mistaking George's deep, sensual tone and she didn't bother to glance over her shoulder.

'Better.' She looked the other way.

'Liar,' he accused softly as she felt his arm brush hers. She shivered involuntarily, instantly responding to the light touch.

'I think I'm a better judge of how my patellar reflexes are doing.' Melody was still finding it hard to look at him. She knew the moment she did, her anger would melt away like snow on a hot summer's day.

'That wasn't what I meant and you know it.'

She could tell he had a smile on that gorgeous mouth of his, even without seeing it. She closed her eyes against the mental image, willing it to go away. It wouldn't. Why was she so in tune with him? Why couldn't she simply switch off her attraction like a light switch?

'Oh?' Melody reluctantly turned to look at him, only to find his face closer than she'd anticipated. 'What was I…' her breath trembled a little but she forced herself to continue. Hold onto the anger, she willed herself. Hold onto the anger '…expected to say? That the visiting orthopaedic surgeon was fondling my leg? That would have gone over brilliantly!'

George chuckled and the sound invaded her heart. She looked away from him but he gently reached over, cupped her chin and urged her face back round. 'Let's get one thing straight.' The taste of his breath held a hint of the red wine they'd been served and Melody savoured it. 'I didn't *fondle* your leg.'

For one blinding second Melody thought he was denying having touched her in the first place. Had he touched her? Had she just imagined it?

'I *caressed* it,' he confessed on a laugh that turned into a groan as he recalled just how perfect she'd felt beneath his touch. 'There's a big difference. One is clumsy but the other is sensual.'

Melody sighed, clinging vainly to her rapidly dissolving anger. 'Well, you still shouldn't have done it.'

'I couldn't help myself.' He shrugged, frowning as he did so.

'Next time try harder!'

'I'm sorry.'

He touched his hand to her shoulder but removed it the instant she glared at him. They were out in public. Anyone might see them talking so intimately together. She edged to the side a little, hoping to put more distance between them.

'I didn't know you were going to react like that. Honestly.'

His tone was so sincere she knew she'd already forgiven him. 'It's all right.' She turned to look out over the city. They were both silent for a few minutes, a comfortable, companionable silence, while they soaked up the beautiful, warm night.

'It's nice here,' he stated. 'In Sydney, I mean.'

'Yeah.'

'How long have you lived here?' Despite the attraction between them, George had to keep reminding himself that he really didn't know Melody all that well.

'In Sydney? About five years now. I attended medical school and did all my training out at Parramatta.'

'Do you like it here? I mean, do you have any plans to leave?'

She shook her head. 'I love it here. I'm close to my brothers, my nieces and nephews and, of course, my parents.'

'Family's important to you?'

'Yes, of course.' Melody paused. 'What about you? Are you close to your sisters?'

'I am. We probably talk about once a month, especially while I've been travelling, but Casey and Rachel talk daily, especially with Rachel in New Zealand.'

'Where does Casey live?'

'She's in Queensland. So are my parents.'

'Oh. Do you have other family in Melbourne?'

He shook his head slowly. 'Veronique's family's in Melbourne. She was born in Sydney but her dad changed jobs and the whole family moved to Melbourne when she was about twelve.'

'Are you close to them?' At the mention of his wife Melody had straightened away from the balcony railing. She kept forgetting he was a widower, a man with experience of what it felt like to be truly loved and accepted by one special person—and that person had been taken from him.

'I'm…' George thought for a moment, as though he was choosing his words carefully. 'They're important to me but… I haven't seen them in almost twelve months.'

'I guess you've had to make a lot of sacrifices this year.' And he'd done it all to carry out his wife's last wishes. Melody took a small step back, starting to realise that, despite what she might be feeling for George, it probably paled in comparison to what he'd shared with his wife. There was no way she'd ever want to compete with his affections for his wife but she had hoped, given the events of this week, that perhaps they were on the verge of a new beginning—for both of them.

'Sacrifices.' He laughed without humour. 'I've made plenty of those.' George looked out at the city lights before them. 'In almost every place I've been I've taken a mental snapshot of the lights, the buildings, the essence of a place, talking to Veronique about what I see and what I'm doing.' He raked a hand through his hair. 'Or at least that's how it started. Then, somewhere along the line, I stopped doing that because I was tired or had to write another lecture or the thousand other things Carmel needs me to do.' His sigh was one mixed with wistfulness and regret. 'I do miss her. So very much.'

'Uh-huh.' Melody wasn't even sure he was aware of her

presence as he seemed to be almost talking to himself. He missed his wife, he was lonely and loneliness could make people do desperate things, like kiss a colleague in the heat of the moment. It made her realise she shouldn't read too much into the personal moments she'd shared with George. He'd be gone in a few days and she'd be here, getting on with her life.

She'd known that all along. At the end of the week George would leave and that would be the end of that. However, that wasn't what she wanted any more. Melody wanted to continue to explore where this burgeoning relationship was headed, to see whether George really was *the one* for her. She'd been so unlucky in love in the past, with both Ian and Emir breaking her heart through their cheating and their lies. Now she'd found a hard-working, open and honest man who could make her insides melt with just one desire-filled glance, and kissed her in a way that no one had ever kissed her before.

Still, there was a streak of distrust in her psyche. If they were to pursue this frighteningly natural chemistry that existed between them, would there come a time in her life when she wouldn't question and double-check everything he'd said to her? She'd believed him when he'd said he didn't have a woman in every port, that she was different, unique and special, but who was to say that wouldn't change after he returned to his life in Melbourne?

He would go back to work, find the natural rhythm of his life again, and he would forget all about the crazy redhead in Sydney who had given him a pleasant momentary interlude. She would be cast aside once again, left to pick up the pieces of her life, because from the way he was talking, the way he was reminiscing about Veronique, his tone clearly radiating his love, Melody started to really get it through her thick, emotional skull that George wasn't ready to move on.

'George! There you are.' Carmel opened the door to the

balcony. 'I've been looking everywhere for you. Several people are asking after you.' It was then Carmel saw Melody standing back from George and she smiled brightly. 'Oh, hey, Melody. I didn't see you there.'

'I was just about to head inside,' Melody stated.

'OK. I just need to go over a few things with George.'

'No problem.'

Carmel held the door for Melody, then turned her attention to George. 'I know you're tired, George, and I know coming to Sydney has probably been one of the more difficult stops on the tour,' Carmel was saying as Melody left the balcony. 'I know Veronique planned for a full day off so she could show you some of her favourite places but we can cut our time here short and—'

Melody didn't want to hear any more. It was time to face facts, to be honest with herself. George couldn't be part of her life, couldn't be part of her future. She had to view this week as being akin to a holiday romance, one pleasant week of diversions, but soon it would be time to return to reality and her reality was here, at St Aloysius, focusing on running the department, treating her patients and concentrating on her research project.

Did it really matter if she was to never marry, to never find the one person she wanted to spend the rest of her life with? Did it really matter if she never had children? Even at the thought, tears began to mist her eyes and she quickly sniffed them away.

The exhaustion of Melody's day—in fact, the combined exhaustion of the entire week so far—began to catch up with her, and when she looked towards the dining room she decided she'd had enough. George needed the time to properly grieve for his wife, to come to terms with his loss, and to do that it meant that she needed to completely remove herself from the equation. Being around her, spending time with her, was probably more of a distraction for George than anything else, despite what he'd told her. Right now, she couldn't be certain George knew what he wanted, and it was up to her to be the strong one and to keep whatever was happening between them on a purely platonic level.

Sadness swamped her at the decision. Not bothering to say goodbye to anyone, she returned to her car and wearily drove home. It was too late for her bubble bath. Once inside, she merely stripped off her glamorous clothes, brushed her teeth and pulled on a pair of boxer shorts and a singlet top before climbing between the sheets and crying herself to sleep.

Once again, she was the one to miss out.

CHAPTER TWELVE

MELODY MANAGED TO concentrate during most of Thursday but as the day wore on the more nervous she became. Had George meant what he'd said? Was he still planning to come around to her place that evening to watch the recordings of her hand and microsurgery reconstructions? Had he only been joking?

She checked her phone several times to see if he'd sent her a message or if she'd missed a call but there was nothing. She knew he had a hectic schedule but surely he could have texted to confirm or something? Perhaps that meant he wasn't coming. The knowledge deflated her.

She'd managed ward round and clinic without a problem, as well as getting a debrief from Andy on the status of Rudy Carlew. So far there had been no complications with his surgery and it looked as though he was going to make an uncomplicated recovery.

'Apparently,' Andy told her, 'he's quite impressed with our Evelyn. He's asked her to stay on as his private nurse for the rest of the movie shoot.'

'Good.' Melody nodded sternly. 'That way we can be sure his arm won't be exacerbated. Evelyn knows what to keep an eye out for.'

'Good heavens, Melody. Don't you see the underlying meaning here?'

'What?' Melody frowned at her registrar, focusing on

his face as his words started to sink in. 'What's the under-lying meaning?'

'That Rudy Carlew and Evelyn are a couple.'

'Really?' Melody was surprised. 'So soon? They hardly know each other.'

'That doesn't matter. When it's the right person, it's just right,' he pointed out. 'That's how it was with me and my wife. Bam!' He clapped his hands together. 'Like a bolt of lightning. Two months later we were married.'

Melody continued to think about what Andy had said for the rest of the day. She had been trying so hard *not* to think about George but perhaps she should? Perhaps she should consider that she'd been struck by lightning! When her phone rang, she immediately hoped it was George, call-ing to let her know whether or not he was coming, but in-stead the image of the caller on her phone screen indicated it was her brother.

'Ethan. How's everything going, big brother?'

'Good. CJ's back at work three and a half days a week and I get two whole days of being Mr Mum to my gor-geous Lizzie-Jean.'

Melody giggled. 'I can't believe you're married with a little girl. After everything you've been through, you fi-nally got your happy ending.' As she was speaking, she felt tears choke her throat.

Before marrying CJ, Ethan had been married to Abigail and expecting his first child, but both his wife and his baby girl had passed away, leaving Ethan almost killing himself with work. Thankfully, Melody's new sister-in-law, who had been left alone and pregnant, had saved her brother. Now the three of them were a family and she couldn't have been happier for them. Everyone was getting their happy ending. Andy had found his wife, even Evelyn had found Rudy Carlew. What about her?

Images of George immediately came to mind and she gasped a little at how readily her thoughts turned to him.

She cared about him and she always would. Closing her eyes, she whimpered as she realised she might have given her heart to a man who might not return her feelings—*again*.

'Mel? Are you OK?' Ethan asked.

'What? Yeah. Why?'

'Because you're whimpering down the phone. What's wrong, sis?'

'Oh…well…everything.'

Ethan chuckled. 'That narrows it down.'

'Uh—I've sort of met someone.'

'Sort of?'

'Remember I told you about the visiting orthopaedic surgeon who was coming?'

'Yeah. A week of lunches, lectures and dinners. You weren't looking—' Ethan stopped. 'You like the VOS?'

'Like? That may be a mild word for the way I feel.'

'What? Wait. What's this guy like? Do Dave and I need to come and meet him? We can come on Saturday and meeting this guy and—'

'Whoa, there, over-protective brother. Steady on.' Melody sighed and told Ethan what had happened over the past few days since George had burst into her life. When she finished, Ethan chuckled.

'It sounds as though you're definitely smitten. I remember feeling like that with CJ. I struggled against it but in the end I came to realise that although we hadn't known each other long, we knew each other deeply. Sometimes, Mel, you just click with people and it sounds as though you've really clicked with George.'

'But what am I supposed to do if he *does* come over tonight to watch these surgeries?'

'If he does come over, Mel, I don't think it's going to be because he wants to watch the surgeries,' Ethan chuckled.

'Why? What does he want to do, then?' She gasped, answering her own question. 'Do you really think he wants to…?' She spoke softly into the phone, a warm blush tinge-ing her cheeks. She was glad she was alone in her office.

'I think he might just want to spend time with you. From what you've said, he seems to be the gentlemanly type. I should know. I'm one.'

'Ha!' Melody teased her brother. 'Seriously, Ethan, what do I do if he *does* just want to—you know, hang out.' She'd only been telling herself just that morning that she wasn't going to get involved with George on anything other than a professional and platonic level, yet even at the thought of George being in her apartment, Melody's body had ignited with desire. The memory of being held close against him, the way his mouth had melded perfectly with her own, the way he could make her forget about absolutely everything when he stared deeply into her eyes…

'What if I get hurt again, Ethan?' she blurted out be-fore her brother could answer. 'I mean, yeah, it's great that I'm putting myself out there again, but do I really want to? Should I? Can I trust my judgement? Is that actually why I've fallen for George, because I know he's unavailable and therefore it's as though I'm doing a pre-emptive strike on getting hurt? Emir didn't want me, so why should George? What if I'm destined to only fall for unavailable men?'

'Oh, sis,' Ethan empathised. 'You're not doing any of those things and Emir was a fool. So was Ian. Both were idiots because any man would be lucky to have someone as awesome as you.'

'You have to say that. You're my brother!'

'Perhaps but you're actually being much braver than before and it does sound as though this George Wilmont guy—who I'm going to investigate online as soon as we've finished this conversation—is a decent fellow and if there's one thing you definitely deserve, it's someone decent.'

Melody forced herself to calm down. 'You're right. And, besides, he might just want to have a platonic evening of watching surgeries.'

'Because we surgeons are quite boring like that,' he joked. 'Look, you like him so use the opportunity to get to know him better. Ask him the burning questions that are no doubt churning through your mind even now, or just let go and enjoy wherever the evening takes you.'

'But he's still in love with his first wife.'

'And he always will be, but it's not a love that's based in the present. It's a love that's based in the past and sooner or later he'll realise that living with ghosts may be detrimental to his health.' Ethan's tone was soft. She knew he was speaking from experience, that he would always have a love for his first wife, but he adored his present wife.

'OK. So I should just enjoy where the evening takes me.'

'Yep.'

'I think I can do that.'

'And remember—forward is good. You told me that.'

'I did, didn't I?'

'Take your own advice, sis. I'd better go. I can hear Lizzie-Jean grizzling for attention.'

'Ooh. Give her a big kiss from her aunty Mel.'

'Will do. Love you, sis.'

'Love you, too, Ethan.'

After she'd ended the call, she sat at her desk and mumbled, 'Forward is good.' She was still telling herself that as she unlocked her front door a few hours later. She'd heard no word from George, so obviously he'd decided not to keep their—their what? Appointment? Date?

She hurried to her room and kicked off her shoes, pulling the clip out of her hair at the same time. Well, if he wasn't coming round, she might be able to finally get that bubble bath she'd promised herself yesterday evening. At least there was no dinner to attend tonight. Still, she'd give him another hour and if he didn't turn up she'd break out the bubbles. Melody changed out of her work clothes into a loose flowing skirt and top, taking time to brush her hair before heading to the kitchen for a drink. She eyed the choice of soothing herbal teas in her cupboard while she waited for the kettle to boil and eventually chose chamomile. She checked the kitchen clock—seven thirty-seven.

'Oh, stop it,' she told herself as she ran a hand through her hair, but the words were easier said than done. She was anxious and on edge. Would he or wouldn't he come? Perhaps she should call him?

When the doorbell rang she jumped in fright, then remained glued to the spot for a whole ten seconds. Was it him? With her heart pounding rapidly, she smoothed her hands down her skirt, telling herself there was nothing to be concerned about, and forced her legs to carry her towards the door.

She opened the door to see George standing there, holding a bottle of wine. 'Hi.' He was wearing a navy polo shirt and the same denim jeans she'd seen him in the other night—the ones that fitted him to perfection. Melody simply stood and stared at him for a long moment, completely forgetting her manners. He was here. 'Can I come in?' he asked slowly, and she finally snapped out of her trance.

'Of course. Of course.' She stepped back to permit him access to her apartment. 'I wasn't sure if you were coming or not.'

'I left a message on your phone.'

'You did?' She frowned as she grabbed her phone and checked. Sure enough, there was a message from George, the time indicating he'd tried to call her while she'd been talking to Ethan. 'Sorry. I didn't get it.'

'Never mind.' He handed her the wine and she turned to take it into the kitchen and put it onto the bench. She knew she needed to pull herself together, she knew she needed to be professional and platonic. Friendship. That's what she could offer him—for now, or at least until she figured out what was really happening between them. 'Would you like a glass now?' She turned to open the overhead cupboard to retrieve glasses.

'No.'

She jumped at the sound of his soft, deep voice from behind her, not realising he'd followed her into the kitchen. When she turned to face him she gasped in surprise. The look in his eyes was unmistakably raw with repressed desire and she parted her lips, her breathing instantly erratic.

His gaze travelled the length of her body, taking in her clothes. 'You look…' He didn't finish the sentence but instead slowly drew closer to her, causing her insides to heat and spiral with warmth. Nothing could have made her look away from him at that heart-stopping moment, and before she could utter a word George hauled her into his arms, his mouth hungrily capturing her own.

In contrast to the kiss they'd shared yesterday, this one was hot and heavy, leaving Melody in little doubt about just how attracted to her George was. So much for the decision to offer a professional and platonic relationship.

His hands roved over her back as he deepened the kiss. She went with him, eager to keep up, eager to show him just how mutual the desire was. He groaned and urged her backwards and soon she felt the coolness of the wall against her back. He leaned in, his body pressing against her own, and she felt her breasts crushed against the firmness of his chest.

The smell of raw, unleashed craving mingled between them as the need for more rose urgently in both of them. She dug her fingers into his shoulder blades before sliding them firmly down his back, feeling the flexed muscles beneath. Wanting to touch him, she impatiently tugged his shirt from the waistband of his jeans, her fingers now itching to make contact with his skin.

When the task was finally completed, she moaned with delight when she reached her objective. His skin was hot to her touch just as she'd known it would be. Giving in to the itch that had been building within her since early Monday morning, she allowed her hands to explore the solid contours of his torso, committing each one to memory.

George groaned against her mouth, unable to believe how this woman could set him on fire. The sensations he was experiencing were all completely foreign but he was definitely enjoying each new one she discovered. The touch of her hands on his body, the way her mouth was responding to his, giving in to every one of his needs, matching them eagerly.

She lifted one leg slightly and coiled it around the back of his, before sliding it slowly down to the floor. The action caused a stirring deep within him and he could feel himself losing control of the situation.

Breaking his mouth free, they both gasped in air before he pushed her hair aside and smothered the smoothness of her gorgeous neck in hot, feverish kisses. He then changed direction and dipped towards the exposed skin above her breasts. Her hands slid out from his shirt at the same time she murmured his name. 'Mmm,' she sighed, lacing her fingers through his hair. 'George.'

The way she said his name pierced right to his heart and he realised that things were getting out of control. He worked his way up, not wanting to break the contact immediately but knowing he must—and soon. He nipped at her ear lobe and she giggled. The sound was intensely provocative and the last thing he needed right now.

He hadn't meant to lose control like that, to grab her and smother her with kisses almost the first instant after he'd walked into her apartment...but she was all he'd been able to think about for most of the day, especially as he hadn't seen that much of her. He'd missed her and his need for her had increased.

'Melody.' With his breathing still out of control, he looked down at her face. Her eyes were closed, her parted lips were dark pink and swollen from his kisses, her breathing as ragged as his own. She was a vision of loveliness.

Unable to resist, he brushed his lips against hers, forcing himself not to deepen the kiss.

'Mmm,' she murmured again, and when he brushed them a third time her hands clamped themselves on either side of his head and held his lips where they belonged. Seductively, she ran her tongue over his lips and was thrilled with the shudder that tore through his body.

Ever so slowly, she kissed him again. Teasing and testing, refusing to deepen the kiss.

'Melody.' This time her name was torn from his lips and she was satisfied with the response.

She kissed him again, not wanting him to speak for she'd already sensed his slow but sure withdrawal. Even though their bodies were still pressed firmly together, George had already mentally distanced himself. She didn't want to think about things rationally and if they stopped completely, then they'd have to talk things through.

Melody just wanted to go on feeling exactly as she was feeling now, not caring about her already bruised heart or the fact that the man in her arms would be leaving within forty-eight hours. She breathed slowly against his mouth before tasting him once again. Now that she knew how incredible they were together, it was something she'd probably crave for the rest of her life.

He didn't break free and he didn't hurry her. Instead, he took what she was offering but held himself under rigid control, still marvelling at how easily he'd lost his perspective. Perhaps the building resistance they'd been employing for the past four days had increased his drive. Whatever this was between them, George knew he'd never experience anything like it again. This was unique for him.

Knowing the moment had come when she couldn't hang onto the physical pull any longer, Melody lowered her hands to his shoulders and slowly opened her eyes. His brown eyes were gazing down into hers, the fire still burning but gradually being doused.

Neither of them spoke but the communication was there. As their breathing steadied to a more normal pace, George reluctantly eased himself away from her. For one fleeting instant he thought Melody might overrule him and drag his body back where it belonged. Instead, she let her hands fall limply to her sides, her gaze dipping briefly to his lips before she looked down at the floor.

He felt awful. How could he have kissed her *again*? He'd already told himself that they would just be friends, colleagues and nothing more. It wasn't fair, to either of them, to torture themselves as they just had. Their lives were running on two completely different tracks. Despite how much he was attracted to her, he also owed her the respect and common decency he would show to other female colleagues. Guilt started to swamp him and he opened his mouth, an apology on his lips.

'Don't.' Melody held up her hand. 'Don't apologise. We both wanted it, we both needed it and we'll both take responsibility for it.'

'You're right, but I was also going to say I never meant it to happen.'

'Liar.' She crossed her arms defensively over her body, rubbing her arms, her body still feeling bereft of his touch. She turned and headed into the living room, leaving him to follow her or stay where he was. She needed to sit down.

'Why am I a liar?' He followed her into the living room. She was sitting with her legs tucked beneath her skirt on a large wingback chair. Her hands were clenched tightly in her lap and her eyes were momentarily closed.

Melody fought for composure before opening her eyes to look at him. 'Because you did mean that kiss to happen. We may not have realised it, but it's been building ever since we met on Monday.' She shrugged, displaying a nonchalance she didn't feel. 'It was…inevitable.'

He registered the truth of her words as he slumped down into the matching chair beside her. 'When you opened the door, I guess everything became too much to control. I was relieved we could see each other without being surrounded by people. I was still trying to resist you because I knew it was the right thing to do, and I was slightly annoyed because you left last night without saying goodbye.' George sighed and shifted in his chair, his gaze intently holding hers.

'Then I had meeting after meeting,' he continued, 'talking to people and presenting information, discussing operating techniques, and the entire time all I could think about was *you*. About seeing you tonight, about being near you, holding you, kissing you.' His gaze dropped to encompass her mouth as he spoke, another thread of desire running through her at such a look. He cleared his throat and eased back in his chair. 'I even snapped at Carmel—twice—and it wasn't even her fault. It was simply because I was behaving like a hormonal, preoccupied teenager.'

'Wow.' She cleared her throat. 'That's, ah, a lot of information to process.'

'We need to be open, to not be afraid to ask questions,' he stated. 'Or answer them.' He reached across, holding out his hand to her, which she accepted. 'Deal?'

Melody felt warmth wash over her at the soft touch from his hand. Open honesty from a man? Was that possible? 'Deal.'

'So…' He gave her hand a little squeeze before releasing it. George settled back in the chair. 'You mentioned you studied in Parramatta?'

'Yes.' Melody smiled. She told him about growing up in that area, about the way her family appreciated vintage cars and her brothers had been over-protective, especially during her teenage years.

George raised his hand and chuckled. 'I understand completely.'

'Hey, you're supposed to be on my side.'

He shook his head. 'As a brother of twin sisters, I'm a card-carrying member of the over-protective brother club.'

'Great. Then you'll get on wonderfully with David and Ethan.'

'I'd like to meet them sometime.' George's words flowed easily from his lips but as he said the words Melody's spine prickled with apprehension.

'Does that mean you're planning on staying in touch after you leave?'

He nodded before shifting in his chair. 'This is why I'm here tonight. To get to know you, to become better friends with you. I don't know what this is, Melody, but I do know it doesn't happen every day.'

'Did it feel that way with—?' She stopped, the question about his wife forming before she'd had time to process it.

'With Veronique?' At her nod, he thought for a moment. 'We were colleagues, then friends, then more than friends, then dating, then engaged, then married.'

'Where are we on that scale?'

'I think we're definitely in the "more than friends" bracket but also in the "friends" and "colleagues" brackets as well.' He stood and walked over to the wall, where there were several pictures of her family as well as framed copies of her medical degrees. 'You and I—we're not doing things in the right order.' He turned to face her.

'I think that's why it's so confusing.'

'Did things happen in the right order with your ex-fiancé?'

'Yes. Colleagues, friends, more than friends. We didn't quite make it to the marriage part.'

'Because he cheated on you?'

'Yes. Several times. With several women, women I still see around the hospital, and there are probably more I still don't know about and don't want to know about.' She sighed heavily.

'It still hurts deeply?'

'Being betrayed? Yes.' Melody angled her head to the side, feeling a wave of emotions she'd thought she'd dealt with rise to the surface. 'With Ian, he flat out lied. He was married, didn't tell me. So that was lying creep number one. A while later, enter lying creep number two who wanted to marry me but with the understanding that he didn't want children.' She sniffed and shook her head slowly from side to side. 'I spent a lot of anxious and soul-searching nights wondering if I could be in a marriage without children and eventually I decided that I could. I could accept that Emir didn't want children, that our careers, the care we had for our patients would be enough.'

'You mentioned he moved to Germany to be with the woman he'd impregnated.'

'Yep.' Tears welled in her eyes. 'It made me realise it wasn't that he didn't want children, it was that he didn't want them with me.' She spread her arms wide then let them drop to her side dejectedly. 'He didn't want me.'

'He really was dead in the head not to want you.' George's words were filled with desire and when she looked at him through her tears she could see by his expression that he meant it.

'Thank you.' She took a tissue from the table and dabbed at her eyes. 'Heartbreak isn't easy but somehow we do survive it.'

'The heart mends. Amazing, eh,' he stated rhetorically.

Melody was quiet for a moment before asking softly, 'How did you feel when you learned of Veronique's death?' George clenched his jaw at the question and Melody quickly held up a hand. 'You don't have to answer th—'

'I felt like dying.'

Melody clutched her hands to her chest, her eyes wide with empathy.

'When I heard the news, I…' He shook his head. 'I wanted to die as well.'

She wanted to go to to him, to hold him, but she stayed

where she was. 'I'm very glad you didn't. Think of all the people you've met during the past year. Think of how many lives you've touched, how many people you've helped, how many lives have been improved. *You've* empowered surgeons around the world to be able to save their patient's lives. That's an amazing legacy, George.'

'And one Veronique wanted for me.'

Melody leaned back in the chair and smiled. 'You've done her proud.'

'You don't mind me talking about her?'

She shook her head, once again realising that George had a lot of things he needed to sort out if there was ever going to be anything developing between them in the future. He was still grieving, still…broken. They both were. 'Veronique was a major part of your life,' she continued. 'We've all loved and lost. Sometimes through heartbreak, sometimes through death and sometimes through both.'

'Both?'

She shrugged. 'My brother, Ethan, went through a difficult time. His wife died from eclampsia and his baby girl died almost a day later. Ethan worked himself into a frenzy and it was only after he had a mild heart attack that he confessed his wife had been drinking heavily during her pregnancy and that his daughter had suffered from foetal alcohol syndrome.'

'The poor man.'

'He's good now. He's found happiness again and a new family.'

'And I'll bet you were his rock, the sister who pulled him through the darkest times of his life.'

'We're a close family.'

'That's nice.' George held her close. 'Family is important. I've realised that more and more this year. At first, I couldn't wait to get away, to leave the hospital where both Veronique and I had worked. Now I have such mixed emotions about going back because I'm not going back to my old life. My old life doesn't exist any more. It's gone and I can never get it back.'

It was that, more than any talk about his wife, which pierced Melody's heart. George wanted his old life back, which only reiterated that he wasn't ready to look to the future and the possibility of a *new* life. Which was why his next words threw her completely.

'Melody—I want to spend together whatever free time we have left. It's only going to be an hour here or half an hour there, I know, but what do you think?'

'Do you think that's wise? Especially given what you've just said?'

'I don't know any more. I don't know what's right or wrong, what might happen or won't happen. I just know that when I'm around you I feel calm and I haven't felt calm in a *really* long time. It's very selfish of me, and you have every right to say no.' He looked expectantly into her face.

She was secretly delighted he wanted to spend time with her but was also highly cautious. 'Well, we both have hectic schedules so it would make it difficult.' She was trying hard to choose her words carefully. She didn't want him to think she didn't want to spend time with him because she did, but she also needed to gauge how much time would be enough for her to hold onto her sanity. Self-preservation was a key factor in her life, especially with her track record of relationships. 'I'll be in Theatre tomorrow, doing the second part of that hand reconstruction, while you'll be doing your last theatre stint of show and tell.'

He chuckled at her wording. 'That's exactly how it feels sometimes.'

She smiled at him. 'We could have breakfast together on Saturday morning before your flight to Melbourne.'

'At the hotel?'

She shook her head. 'I know a nice all-day breakfast place I'd like to take you to.' They could say a private goodbye and then she could come home and cry her heart out.

'You'll pick me up?'

'Sure. Then I can take you straight to the airport.' Even as she said the words she wasn't sure it was the best idea but he was right when he'd said they had very little time to spend together.

'It's a date.' The way he looked at her, with a mixture of need, want and desire, left her with little doubt as to how she affected him. He clenched his jaw and shoved his hands into his pockets, as though to keep himself from crossing to her side and gathering her close.

They stared at each other for so long she was about to capitulate and cross to his side, eager to have his mouth on hers once more. George cleared his throat. 'We'd better start watching these brilliant reconstructive surgeries of yours before I lose all control.'

'Wait.' His words took a second or two for her sluggish brain to process. 'You were serious about that?'

'Yeah. I really am interested.' He pulled a USB memory stick from his pocket. 'The library downloaded the files onto this stick for me and told me to keep it.'

'You are really strange if your idea of fun is to sit and watch recordings of surgeries.' She took the stick from him and put it into the USB port at the rear of her television. Soon they were sitting on the lounge facing the television ready to watch the surgery. 'Are you sure?' she checked one last time as he put his arm down the back of the lounge, his body very close to hers. It was exciting and comforting and sexy to have him so near. If this was her holiday romance, she couldn't think of anything better to do on a date. Watching surgery with another surgeon, someone who really understood her work.

'I want to spend time with you, Melody, and tonight this is all the time I have. I don't think either of us are emotionally ready for the result our attraction could provide, so...' He took the remote from her and pressed 'play'. 'If this is the way I get to spend time with you, then so be it.'

'OK, but it goes for over four hours.'

'If I get bored, which I seriously doubt, I'll fast-forward and you can provide me with a commentary about what I've missed.'

'Oh, joy.' Melody couldn't help but laugh at his serious-ness on the issue.

'Also, can we order some food? I'm starved.' He kicked off his shoes and pulled out his phone. 'What do you feel like eating? Noodles? Curry? Pizza?'

'Er…curry?' She marvelled at how relaxed and at home he seemed. He was probably so sick and tired of living out of a hotel that being at a real home was probably some-thing of a novelty. He ordered some food, told her it would be delivered in half an hour, then snuggled closer to watch Melody performing surgery.

They both watched as the operating theatre came into focus and there she was, standing at the operating table, explaining the finer points of what she was about to do. She felt self-conscious watching herself, never having sat through a viewing of the recording before, but with George asking questions she found herself reaching for the remote to pause it while they discussed things in more detail.

It was liberating to be able to sit down with a man and discuss a subject she was passionate about. He seemed to be really interested and the knowledge thrilled her. It was wonderful and exhilarating, as well as desperate and sad. Here she was, bonding with a man who would leave her in forty-eight hours.

CHAPTER THIRTEEN

HER NECK HURT. As the pain sent signals to her brain Melody shifted slightly but the pain continued. It felt as though someone was pinching her neck and she wished they'd stop. It was a mosquito, she realised, and swatted it away. No. The pain was still there.

Slowly, she was drawn out of the dream state to reality. The pain in her neck still there and annoying. She must be sleeping at an odd angle. She shifted slightly, only to come up against a hard obstacle.

Had she left her books on the bed again? She kicked at them with her leg but they didn't fall. She kicked them harder, only to hear them groan. Groan! Books didn't groan! Melody frowned. She felt with her foot and realised with a start that it wasn't a book but a leg!

Her eyes snapped open and she tried desperately to focus. She was in her lounge room, the television still on. She was lying against the back of the lounge suite, her legs entwined with George's, his arm holding her possessively to his body. George! Oh, no. They'd been watching her reconstruction recordings and had fallen asleep.

She scrambled into an upright position, shaking him fiercely. 'Wake up.' She shook him. 'George. Wake up.' With the tiny beams of light peeking from behind her thick curtains, she guessed it to be quite early in the morning.

'Huh?' He slowly moved, stretching languorously. Melody was pierced with longing as she watched him. His body was lean and hard, muscles tensing firmly before relaxing. His leg brushed hers, igniting a spark she'd been trying to repress ever since he'd arrived last night. He shifted to a sitting position beside her and peered blearily into her eyes.

'Mmm.' With his eyes half-closed, he leant over and kissed her soundly on the mouth. 'Hi, there.' His voice was deep and low. 'Guess we must have dozed off.' He reached for her, gathering her into his arms. She resisted him but only slightly. He nuzzled her neck. 'You're a cuddly girl at heart, aren't you?'

Melody smiled. The embarrassment from their impromptu night on the lounge faded a little. How could she resist when he said such nice things?

He pointed to the TV. 'How long did you say that last recording went on for?'

'They're all about four hours and we did watch two—or was it three? We started the second one after we'd finished eating, I remember that.'

George laughed, a deep rumbling sound that warmed her. 'I guess it doesn't really matter. Besides, I think we were both exhausted.'

'It has been an incredibly hectic week,' she replied as she went to move from his arms.

'Where are you going?'

'To grab the remote.' She pointed to where the remote had fallen off the table onto the floor.

'Wait.' He shifted to the right and, sticking his leg out to the side, he managed to bring it closer. 'Almost got it.' He reached over further before crowing triumphantly as he snatched it up into his hand. 'Done.' He pointed it at the set and turned it off.

It was then Melody noticed the clock on the wall. 'What? That can't be right.' She scrambled for her mobile phone and checked the time. 'Ten to eight! I'm due at work in ten minutes.'

Melody sprang from his arms and rushed out the room. Moments later, George could hear the shower running. He shook his head. Carmel must be having a hissy fit. He grimaced as he stood, stretching his cramped muscles again before pulling his phone from his pocket. He'd purposely put it on silent all night, not wanting to be disturbed. Sure enough, there were several missed calls from Carmel and even more text messages.

With a reluctant sigh he called Carmel back. 'Carmel,' he said into the receiver when she answered. A split second later he held the phone away from his ear as Carmel's voice boomed through. 'Calm down,' he tried. It didn't work. He heard the shower stop and realised that Melody was going to be leaving her house very soon. As he'd come in a taxi last night, he had no way of getting back to his hotel—well, no way that wouldn't take another half an hour or more. She'd have to give him a lift.

'Carmel,' he said finally, 'you're wasting time. What's my schedule?' He listened intently, his mind working overtime. 'All right. Bring me a change of clothes and a clean suit. I'll meet you in the theatre block.' He could at least have a shower and change there. He disconnected the call then headed to the kitchen, his stomach grumbling as he checked the contents of Melody's fridge.

A few minutes later she came rushing into the kitchen while he finished his orange juice and bit into an apple. 'Can I get you anything?' he asked.

'Yes. Get out of my apartment!'

'Not a problem. Which way is your car?'

'What?' Melody exploded. 'You can't come to work with me.'

'Why not? I need to go to the hospital. You're going there. What's the problem?'

She looked at him as though he'd grown an extra head. 'The problem, Professor, is that everyone will see you coming to work in my car and as you're dressed in casual clothes, they'll put two and two together and make four!'

'So?'

Melody threw her hands up in exasperation. 'Typical of you. You'll be gone tomorrow and I'll have to live with the rumours and gossip—*again*.' She didn't have time for this. She reached into the fridge and pulled out a banana before storming from the kitchen, George hard on her heels.

'It's not fair,' she continued to mutter. 'Not to my emotions, not to my neurotic thought processes and not to my anxiety, all of which are flaring right now and blending themselves in a fine state.' Her voice broke at the end and she sniffed, doing her best to keep herself under control. She needed to drive. She needed a clear head and yet with George being so close to her, being so insistent, she was finding it difficult to get her thoughts in order. Of course, what he said made perfect, logical sense but emotionally being in the car with him and driving to the hospital first thing in the morning was increasing her irrational levels to maximum.

'This is different and you know it. Nothing happened last night.'

'You know that and I know that but the fact remains that we'll be seen arriving together and you'll be leaving tomorrow.'

'What am I supposed to do?'

'Call a taxi and wait.'

'I can't. I'm lecturing at eight.'

'Then you're going to be late, no matter what you do.' She stormed towards her car, which was located in the communal garage. 'Look, George, I've spent a lot of time picking up the pieces of my life since Emir left and I'm not about to give the people at St Aloysius the chance to give me pitying looks accompanied by not-so-quiet whispers behind my back as I walk past them.'

'Melody, you're overreacting. Besides, what does it matter what people say about you? Surely you're above all that.'

Melody was filled with temper and frustration, and at his comment she wanted to throw something at him. 'You just don't get it, do you? I don't care what people think. They respect me as a surgeon and a professional, but there's only so much gossip and speculation a girl can take, George, and right at the moment I don't choose to take any more.' She'd unlocked her car and noticed that George was determined to get in. He sat beside her as she revved the engine and reversed.

'Drop me a block before the hospital and I'll walk the rest of the way,' he told her quietly, and she started to feel silly about her tirade.

She sighed with resignation. 'Listen, I'm sor—'

'No.' He held up his hand. 'It's fine. You don't need to apologise.'

Although his words sounded sincere, the strained silence that followed made Melody realise that things had just changed—again. She shook her head as she pulled to the kerb a block away from the hospital. His smile was forced when he climbed out and started walking. This week had been a mix of exhaustion and exhilaration and as she drove away from him, glancing at him in her rear-vision mirror, she felt a sense of loss.

'What is *wrong* with you? You're behaving like a complete nut case and all because he needed a lift and you didn't want to be gossiped about.' She reached her designated parking spot. 'It's not as though George is anything special, just a holiday romance, an interlude. Nothing more, yet you're behaving as though you're completely smitten with him.' As she spoke the words out loud to her empty car she gasped. Turning off the engine, she covered her hands with her face and shook her head. 'No. No, no, no, no, no. You are *not*.'

She shoved the thoughts away, but they refused to budge.

'No. You are not in love with him. You are *not*.' But even as she denied it to herself, the truth seemed to slap her in the face. She didn't want to be in love with George Wilmont. 'Nope. I refuse.' She dropped her hands, straightened her shoulders and climbed from the car.

After locking it, she headed towards her office on legs that felt all stiff and uncooperative. *You're in love, you're in love, you're in love*, the rhythm of her steps seemed to state. 'No, I'm not, no, I'm not, no, I'm not,' she mumbled softly to herself, but even when she denied it, she knew it was true.

She was in love with George and not in the way she'd been in love before. Oh, no. This was the *real* thing. With Emir she'd felt secure and safe, yet with George she *needed* him just as she needed oxygen to breathe. He'd become a part of her. A vital, desperate part and one she couldn't bear to be without—yet she had to.

Somehow she managed to pull herself together and concentrate on work. She managed to make it in time for ward round and then headed to Theatre. The second part of the hand reconstruction went extremely well and the success of the operation did much to bolster her failing spirits.

She didn't get time to see George as between an emergency case and a full clinic she was swamped for the rest of the day. That night she dressed carefully in the last outfit she'd bought for her week as host to the visiting orthopaedic surgeon. It was his official farewell dinner and she wanted to look perfect. She was desperate to see that spark of desire in his eyes again, at the same time dreading the thought of seeing that blank, professional look he reserved for people he didn't know well.

Her dress was two-tone, the bodice made from navy velvet and the skirt from pale blue silk. A wide band of navy velvet circled the base of the skirt and Melody had never felt more pretty in a dress than she did in this one. She was glad she'd saved it for last.

She took time with her hair, piling half of it up and leaving the other half to swirl around her shoulders. There was no need for a necklace as the dress had a high neckline. Finally, pleased with her appearance, she drove to the venue. Once again, she noted she was seated at George's table and called on every last ounce of determination she had, knowing she would need it to get through the night.

The instant she saw him across the crowded room her stomach began to churn and her knees went weak. She propped her elbow up on the bar for support and as her mouth went dry she reached, with a not-so-steady hand, for her drink. It was true. It was really true. She hadn't been imagining it after all. She really was in love with George Wilmont.

He spotted her and, just as she'd known, his brown eyes darkened momentarily with repressed desire. He quickly returned his attention to the person talking to him but she could see his impatience in the way he stood, the way he smiled politely and the way his gaze flicked to her another three times in under thirty seconds.

'Wow, boss,' Andy remarked from beside her. 'You look great.'

'Thank you, Andy,' she responded, smiling at her registrar as they were called into dinner. 'As do you.' He offered her his arm and she took it. She wanted to walk in with George, to talk with him, listen to him, soak up everything about him—but at the same time she wanted to keep as far away from him as possible.

It was just too soon. She'd only realised that morning that she was in love with the man and, quite frankly, she needed some time to adjust. Melody wasn't sitting next to George this time, which brought more mixed emotions. She wanted to be next to him, feel his body close to hers, breathe in the irresistible scent of him, fight the pull of his hypnotic gaze, and at the same moment she was glad of the reprieve.

Andy sat on one side of her, with Mr Okanadu on the other, his wife next to him. Mrs Okanadu spoke animatedly about her grandchildren and although Melody smiled and nodded in the right places, she was always conscious of every move George made.

He was seated almost directly opposite her and their gazes clashed several times across the large round table. Just after the main meal Melody excused herself and headed to the rest rooms. Once there, she leaned against the wall for support and closed her eyes. He was gorgeous, sexy and far too close. It pained her that he would leave tomorrow and right now, when she should be making the most of the time they had left together, she was keeping as far away as she possibly could.

'Hi, there.'

Melody's eyes snapped open at the other woman's voice and she found herself face to face with Hilary, one of the theatre nurses. 'Feeling all right?' she asked as she repaired her bright red lipstick.

'Sure,' Melody replied. 'Just a bit tired.'

'I hear the hand reconstruction went well.'

'Yes.' Melody nodded quickly. 'Very well.'

Hilary paused and looked over her shoulder before saying, 'I also hear that you and a certain visiting surgeon have been spending quite a bit of time together.'

Melody didn't need to look in the mirror to know that the colour had just drained from her face. 'Wh-what do you mean?'

'I mean the fact that I saw him get out of your car this morning a block away from the hospital, and I wasn't the only one.' She grinned wildly at Melody. 'So—what's he like?'

'Like?'

'You know, to kiss? To cuddle? In bed?'

Melody's jaw dropped open in shock. 'That's none

of your business.' The instant the words were out of her mouth, she realised she'd incriminated herself.

'So you *are* involved. How romantic! Was I right? Is he divorced or is he just…lonely?'

'Oh, this isn't happening,' Melody mumbled as she turned on the cold tap and ran her hands beneath the water. Taking a deep breath and calling on every ounce of professionalism she could muster, she turned off the tap and dried her hands before answering. 'Look, George is a nice man.'

'No kidding.'

'We're colleagues. *That's all.*'

'Yeah, right. I saw him get out of your car at eight o'clock in the morning. I know which hotel he's staying at, and you were coming from the opposite direction. I was also at his lecture, which started late, and when he finally arrived he was dressed in a suit and his hair was wet, as though he'd just had a shower.'

Melody gulped over the hard lump in her throat. She hated being the subject of hospital gossip and she knew that losing her temper and giving the nurse a piece of her mind would do no good. She was caught between a rock and a hard place—again—and, as usual, the guy walked away with no repercussions. Hilary was waiting for her answer and Melody smiled politely.

'You're a great theatre nurse.'

The other woman frowned. 'As opposed to what?'

'A private eye.' Melody turned on her heel and walked out. Inside, she was shaking like a leaf and thanked her training for making her appear outwardly composed. She tried telling herself she didn't care about the rumours and gossip but it didn't work. She should have made him take a taxi. She should have known that one block from the hospital wouldn't have been sufficient distance for people not to see them together.

'Shoulda, coulda, woulda…' she muttered as she walked over to the now deserted bar and leaned against it. What was she going to do? The pitying glances, the sorrowful looks. They were all going to come again, along with the 'poor Melody' sighs. This time, though, it would tear her heart to shreds and she doubted she'd ever recover.

Tears started to well in her eyes and she willed them away, massaging her temples, trying desperately to get herself under control. She sniffed and realised she was fighting a losing battle. She bit her lip and closed her eyes, tears falling onto her cheeks that she gently brushed away as she concentrated on some deep breaths.

'There you are.' George's deep voice washed over her. 'I've been worried.'

Her heart lunged with happiness at his words, making her feel as though everything would turn out right. He'd been worried about her. He'd been conscious of the time she'd been away from the table. Here was the man she loved, being so—so—darn sweet and yet, as she stared into his face, she couldn't help be swamped with overwhelming anger.

'What's wrong?' he asked when he saw she was upset. George went to place a hand on her shoulder but she quickly stopped him.

'Don't.'

'What's wrong?' he repeated, his tone more cautious than before.

'People saw you getting out of my car this morning.'

'What?' His eyes were wide with shock.

Melody shook her head. 'I knew I should have made you take a taxi.'

'So this is all my fault?'

'Yes.'

'How do you figure that?'

'Because you'll be gone tomorrow.'

'So?'

'So I'm the one who's going to be left with the rumours, gossip and pitying looks.'

'And you think you're the only person who's ever been gossiped about in hospitals?' George shoved both hands into his trouser pockets and looked down at his shoes for a moment. Slowly he lifted his head. 'I had to endure everything and more when Veronique died. She was an admin assistant there, so not only did I get pitying looks and sympathy, left, right and centre, I also had to deal with people avoiding me because they didn't know what to say. For six months, until I left to come away on the VOS, people avoided me. I didn't have normal conversations with my theatre staff except for "Pass me that retractor"!' He spoke in a harsh whisper, one that cut through Melody's self-indulgence like a scalpel.

'In some ways it was a relief to leave. I could concentrate on work, forget my pain and not have to put up with the quiet whispers in the hospital corridors. So, Dr Janeway, you are not the only one to have encountered the horrible hospital grapevine.'

Melody nodded once, acknowledging his words. 'But I can't escape,' she said softly. 'This is where I'm employed and although I plan to focus on my research, I still have to be Acting Director until the hospital appoints a successor. *This* is the hospital where I've been gossiped about before. It may not have been of the magnitude of yours but, still, the words, the looks—they can really hurt and I'm sick of it happening.' Her words were calm as she gazed up at him. She dabbed the tears from her eyes.

'Melody, I—'

'I'm going home now.'

He gazed at her for a long, drawn out moment and the whole world seemed to slip away, leaving the two of them the only people on earth. They'd connected. In five long, hectic days they'd made a dramatic connection and one where Melody had fallen madly in love with the man in front of her.

She wanted him to hold her, to kiss her, to tell her that

everything would be all right. She wanted him to comfort her, to tell her she was important to him and that he loved her. She wanted—she wanted things he couldn't give.

George nodded and stepped back. 'I'll make your apologies.'

'I'd appreciate it.' Melody forced her legs to work as she walked past him.

'Can we still meet for breakfast tomorrow morning?' He spread his hands wide, indicating the decision was hers.

'Yes.'

'Good. I want a chance to say a proper goodbye.'

She opened her mouth to speak but closed it again, unsure what she should say. Goodbye? Why did everything seem so final with that word?

'Sleep sweet, Melody.' As much as he wanted to scoop her up and kiss her senseless, George knew he couldn't. He clamped down on the feeling, knowing it wouldn't do him any good. He'd just have to cool his heels until tomorrow. He watched the way she walked, head held high, purse clutched tightly in her hand. Her hips swayed slightly, her shoulders back, and he felt a tightening in his gut. She was dazzling and she'd dazzled him all week long.

Even as he allowed himself to acknowledge these feelings, hard on their heels came ones of guilt and remorse. He knew he was legally a free man, but mentally and emotionally George wasn't sure if he was ready to move on. No matter what he did, he would end up hurting Melody. He cared about her so much that the thought of causing her pain made him feel physically ill.

If—and it was a big if—there was going to be anything permanent between Melody and himself, he owed it to both of them to deal with his past first, before moving on to the future. For the present? He raked a hand through his hair. For the present he was going to enjoy her company one last time. The consequences, for both of them, would come later. Of that he had little doubt.

CHAPTER FOURTEEN

ON SATURDAY MORNING he met her at the front of the hotel. Carmel would be taking his luggage to the airport so he wouldn't need to worry about it. Instead, he could focus on enjoying Melody's company as she drove them to her favourite café.

'What did you tell Carmel?' she asked him as they sat opposite each other and perused the menus.

'I told her you and I were going out for breakfast.'

'Really? What did she say?'

'She said, "Good."' He shrugged one shoulder. 'She thinks it's good for me to move forward with my life.'

Melody silently thanked Carmel for encouraging George. 'If breakfast is a step forward, then I'm glad to share it with you.' She grinned and reached for his hand.

'This is our last opportunity to be together.' He took her hand in his and raised it to his lips. 'Let's enjoy it.' They ordered food and enjoyed a leisurely meal. 'It's great not having to rush anywhere,' George remarked as he eased back in his chair and sipped his coffee. 'It's great just being with you.'

'I know what you mean.' Melody smiled, holding her coffee cup out to him. He clinked it and they both laughed. She didn't want to talk about their impending separation, about what might happen tomorrow or the next day or the day after that. She needed to savour, memorise, absorb every detail about George.

However, when they could delay their departure no longer, Melody concentrated on the road as she navigated her way towards the frantic Sydney airport, the soothing strains of Mozart filling the car.

George rested his head, eyes closed as the music surrounded them. His internal thoughts were turbulent, his emotions jumbled up and out of control. Meeting Melody had thrown his neatly ordered world into disarray and he wasn't sure how to put it back. He didn't want to leave her but he knew he had to go. He wanted to kiss her, to hold her close, but every time he did so he was later visited by guilt for moving on from his memories of Veronique.

He wanted to tell Melody that she meant a lot to him, that he wanted to be with her, to investigate this attraction, but he couldn't. He couldn't because he wasn't sure. He wasn't sure he wanted to be involved in another serious relationship. He'd loved deeply once before and his world had been blown apart when Veronique had died. Was he ready to put himself out there again? To risk loving another woman?

When Melody pulled into the airport car park she didn't turn the engine off. Instead, she swivelled in her chair and looked at him. His heart skipped a beat as he stared into her gorgeous green eyes. How was it possible she could have such a dramatic effect on him? When he saw tears beginning to gather in her eyes, his heart almost broke at the thought of leaving her.

'Uh—are you OK to go from here?'

'You're not going to walk me in?'

She shook her head. 'I don't know if I can.' Melody gazed into his eyes, her stomach churning with butterflies while her lower lip trembled.

He unbuckled his seat belt then reached out and cupped her face in his hands. 'Melody.' Her name was a caress on his lips before his mouth met hers in a hungry, fiery and consuming kiss. He never wanted it to end. He wanted to take her with him, for her to be with him for ever. Melody moaned in delight, giving everything she had to him, and, being greedy, he took it.

His phone beeped, indicating he'd received a text message. 'It's Carmel. She says they're calling our flight.' He opened the car door and climbed out, pleased when Melody climbed from the driver's seat and came around to him.

'Will you walk me in?' He just couldn't leave her—not yet. But why? Why was he finding it so difficult to say goodbye?

'I'll walk you to the door but I just— I can't…' She stopped and took his hand in hers. 'I can't watch you walk away from me.'

George shook his head and gathered her close once more. 'I know. I finally understand Shakespeare's "Parting is such sweet sorrow."' He kissed Melody again but when another text message came through, he knew if he didn't hustle, he'd miss the plane. 'I've got to go.'

She held his hand for a moment longer and shook her head, not bothering to choke back the tears. 'George…' She shook her head. 'I—I don't want you to go.' Her words were broken as the emotion burst forth. He clenched his jaw and shook his head before gathering her close and kissing her deeply one last time. 'I—I love you, George.'

He leaned back and looked at her in utter astonishment. She *loved* him? Before he could process her words, his name was called over the PA system.

'I have to go.'

She hiccupped a few times, letting him go and covering her mouth with her hand. He forced himself to turn, to walk away from her, and with each step he felt as though he was walking through a quagmire. He told himself not to look back but just before he was rushed through security he gave in to the impulse and what he saw almost broke his own heart.

There she was. The woman who had just offered him her love, standing alone near the doorway, hands covering her face as she sobbed. She loved him. Melody *loved* him—and he was leaving. He had to. He had to return to Melbourne to find out what his life was all about because right at this moment he really had no clue.

Who was he? How could he let go of the past? What was he supposed to do when the tour ended? He shook his head sadly as he continued through the process of boarding the plane, barely hearing a word Carmel or anyone else said. How had he reached a point in his life where he had no earthly idea what he was doing? Could he ever hope to be happy again, or was he doomed to the loneliness that stretched before him?

Lonely widower George Wilmont. Was that all?

CHAPTER FIFTEEN

WHEN THE DOORBELL RANG, George walked through his house, a slight spring in his step. He opened the door with anticipation and smiled at Carmel. 'I never thought I'd be happy to see you at my door,' he stated, and Carmel laughed. 'Come in.' He beckoned.

'Would it be crazy to say I've missed you?' she asked as she followed him through to the dining room, which was strewn with papers. 'I can't believe it's almost two whole weeks since we finished the tour.'

'I can't believe I've written so many reports and papers in those two weeks.'

'Are they all finished?'

'Ah…there's that Miss Efficient Organiser tone I haven't missed at all.' They both laughed and sat down to chat.

'How are you doing, George?' She gestured to the sparse room. 'I mean, Christmas is two days away and not a decoration in sight.'

He shrugged. 'Not really in the Christmas spirit this year.'

'Are you doing anything on Christmas Day? Seeing Veronique's family?'

He shook his head. 'I'm rostered on at the hospital.'

'I didn't think you were back there until the New Year.'

'I'm just doing a few shifts over the Christmas and New Year period. The acting head of department needs to spend some time with his family.' Even as he said the words 'acting head of department' his thoughts immediately went to a different acting department head, a beautiful redhead with mesmerising green eyes who had captured his heart.

Ever since leaving Sydney to complete the visiting orthopaedic specialist tour, George had been hard pressed to get Melody out of his head. Two days after they'd left he'd received an official email from her, on behalf of the rest of the department, thanking him and his staff for choosing St Aloysius as part of the VOS tour. It had been formal, official and he'd been miserable on reading it. Melody. He couldn't go to sleep without thinking of her smile, without dreaming of being with her, laughing with her, kissing her.

'You're like a bear with a sore head,' Carmel had accused him five days later. 'For heaven's sake, email Melody, call Melody, text her with a plethora of emojis if you're unsure what to say, but do *something*, George. You're making the rest of us miserable.'

And so he'd emailed her, an equally polite message, stating that he and his team had enjoyed their stay. He'd signed off the email asking her what her favourite part had been. He'd received a one-word reply—*You*. Clearly that hadn't been an official email but the reply had made his heart soar with delight, and along with the delight had come the guilt, the guilt that he was moving on from his marriage, that he was moving away from Veronique and everything they'd shared together.

Since then, he'd taken Carmel's advice on board and had sent Melody a text message with emojis. His usual one had been the exhausted or sleeping emoji. She would often reply with emojis of her own, all of them upbeat and encouraging, as though she was eager for him to finish this tour.

Carmel waved a hand in front of his face. 'I know that blank look. You were thinking about Melody, weren't you?'

George sighed, not bothering to deny it. 'She's constantly on my mind. I don't know what to do.'

'Do you love her?'

'I…' He shrugged his shoulders and closed his eyes. 'I don't know. Sometimes I think yes, sometimes I think no. Sometimes I think we had such an intense time together, it must all have been an illusion. Perhaps there's nothing more between us than infatuation?'

'That doesn't sound like fun.'

'It isn't. That's why I was more than happy to pick up a few shifts at the hospital. Work will help.'

'That's what you told me after Veronique's death. Work would help.'

'And it did. It always does.'

'But you also run the risk of working too much, of burying your life in work and then having nothing else to exist for.' Carmel's words held a hint of sadness and nothingness. It helped snap George out of his own self-pity.

'Are you and Diana OK?'

'We're more than OK.' Carmel held up her hand to reveal a lovely engagement ring.

'Wow!' George inspected the ring. 'That's beautiful.'

'Diana chose it. I chose hers. We're very happy, George, but I was so caught up in my work for so long that I didn't see how happy I could be if I just let myself.'

'Are you telling me to let myself be happy? Because if you are, I'm not sure I know how to do that.'

Carmel thought for a moment then changed the subject. 'How's Veronique's family?'

'They're good. Great even. Her parents have travel plans, her sister's pregnant.'

'Good for them.'

'Everybody's moving on.' He shook his head. 'In some ways it's as though we're forgetting Veronique altogether.'

'No.' Carmel shook her head. 'Not *forgetting*, George, but honouring her by not weeping or covering yourself with sackcloth and ashes for the rest of your life. You know she wouldn't have wanted that. She would have wanted you to be happy.'

'That's what her mother told me.'

'It's good advice.'

'But how do I do that?' He spread his arms wide, indicating the house. 'Even this place feels like it belongs to someone else.'

'It did. You're a different man now, George. You're not Veronique's husband any more.'

'No. I'm not that man.'

'You're a new man, with a new world at your command. So the big question is, what do you want? Where do you want to live? Do you want to work at Melbourne General? Who do you choose to share your life with?'

They were definite questions to think on, and after Carmel had collected all the reports and papers and said her farewells, George walked back into his quiet house and sat staring at his phone. Every question he asked himself seemed to lead to one person—and one person only. Melody. He should call her. He should—

His phone beeped. It was a message from Melody. Three emojis—a happy face, a Christmas tree and a heart. He raised his eyebrows at the heart. That was one she'd never sent him before. A heart? Did that mean she still loved him? He hadn't quashed it by not professing his own feelings?

Was it possible that he could be twice blessed in love? First with Veronique and now with the vivacious, intelligent and heart-melting Melody Janeway?

Love? Was he in love with Melody? Even as the question crossed his mind, he couldn't help the large smile that spread across his lips.

Melody put her phone on the table and closed her eyes. She shouldn't have sent him the heart emoji. It was too much. They hadn't even spoken since he'd left, just the initial emails and then text messages consisting of emojis. It was silly but it was better than nothing, and if that's what George needed to do while he figured out what he wanted then she would wait.

It was a decision she'd come to about three days after he'd left Sydney. Her brother Ethan had come to Sydney with a patient and had insisted on having a frank discussion with his little sister.

'You're clearly in love with the man,' Ethan had stated after she'd told him everything.

'I know.'

Ethan had chuckled. 'And yet you don't sound too happy about it.'

'There's nothing I can do, Ethan, but wait. George has a lot to sort out, more emotional baggage than I have, I think. The death of his wife is a far greater loss to deal with than a broken engagement by some jerk I'm better off without.'

'So you're just going to wait?'

'I'm going to *hope*.'

'Hope is good but it'll only get you so far, Mel. One day you'll need to act because if you don't, you risk losing everything. Believe me, I know. I was almost too stubborn to let go of my past so that I could move forward with CJ and now...' he'd grinned '... I'm the happiest man on earth.'

'That's what I want. I want to be happy—*with George*.'

'Does this mean you're thinking about moving to Melbourne?'

She'd sighed and nodded. 'If I have to, yes.'

'Huh. Surprising but good. Or would you prefer George to move to Sydney?'

'I don't care if we both move and end up in Far North Queensland or overseas, I just want to be with him, Ethan. I love him.' Her job was to wait and hope and pray and love George from afar, giving him the space he needed so he could sort out what he wanted. Melody hoped it was her.

* * *

Melody spent her Christmas working at the hospital and even though there weren't too many patients in the wards and all the hospital administrative meetings had been cancelled until the new year, she was glad of the opportunity to lose herself. Thinking about George every hour she was awake and then dreaming about him all night was almost becoming exhausting. Almost…

Two days after Christmas, though, the CEO had told her to take time off work. 'Go home, Melody. See your family. Go and see your new niece and spend some time with Ethan in the wine district. You're starting to look as ashen as he used to.'

'But there's so much to do,' she'd protested, but had been overruled.

'And there will be plenty of time to do it,' she'd been told in return. 'This request is not negotiable.'

And so Melody had headed to see Ethan and CJ for the New Year, delighting in spending time with Lizzie-Jean, who was crawling all over the place and starting to pull herself up on furniture. She watched her brother and CJ together, amazed at just how happy Ethan really was, and she yearned to be equally as happy.

She'd received the usual text message emojis from George, the exhausted or sleepy one and—on Christmas Day—a Christmas tree with a smiley face. Had she been wrong to send him the heart emoji? Had she scared him off?

It was only two days into the new year when her phone rang and she quickly checked the caller identification— her heart plummeting when she realised it was only the hospital's CEO.

'Melody, I'm sorry to call you but we actually need you to come back to the hospital.'

'What's wrong?'

'Nothing's wrong,' the CEO told her. 'We've found the perfect candidate to take over from you as head of department. Isn't that great news?'

'It is. Do you need me to come back and do a handover?'

'That's exactly what we need. If you can have one week with the new head, handing things over while the operating lists and patient numbers are low, that would be helpful. Then, when clinics start up in another week, he'll be ready to take on the full duties and you'll be free to return to your position as resident orthopaedic surgeon and devote as much time to your research project as you'd like.'

Melody breathed in a cleansing breath. It also meant she'd be able to move to Melbourne if she needed to.

'Who's the new head, then?' Ethan asked, as he watched his sister pack.

'I didn't ask and I don't really care.' She laughed with delight. 'I'm free, Ethan. I don't have to worry about letting everyone down and I can move to Melbourne to be near George and—'

'What happened to giving him space?'

'I think he's had enough space. I'm through marking time. I'm going to find that man and make him see sense. I'm going to let him know that I love him and I'll wait for as long as I need to until he can tell me he loves me, too because I'm pretty sure he does…' She frowned. 'At least, I hope he does.'

'Don't go second-guessing yourself,' Ethan encouraged as he zipped up her bag and carried it out to her car. 'It's not that I want you to leave, sis, but, seriously, go and get this whole thing sorted out so I can see you being happy instead of being as miserable as a wet week.'

Melody laughed, not taking offence at her brother's words. It was because he loved her, because he wanted the best for his sister that he was all but pushing her out of his home.

The drive back to Sydney was refreshing as she started making plans for her new future.

She hadn't realised how much of a weight the head of department job had been around her neck until it had been lifted. When she arrived at her apartment, it was to find George standing there, knocking on her door.

Melody closed her eyes and blinked one very long blink as she continued to stare at him. Was she seeing things?

'George?'

He turned to look at her, taking in the bag in her hand and the sunglasses on her head. 'You weren't home.'

'No. I was at Ethan's.'

'Oh. I didn't know.'

'How could you?'

They stood there, so close to each other and yet so far apart, both of them having the most ridiculous conversation as they drank in the sight of each other. 'What are you doing here?'

'I—uh—sent you a text message.'

'You did?' She dug in her bag for her phone. 'I have it off when I drive so I'm not tempted to answer any calls or messages.'

'Good. Safe driving practice,' he stated. 'That's good.'

She found her phone and switched it on, waiting impatiently for the message light to blink so she could look at it. When she opened the text message from George it was to find one single emoji—a red heart.

Melody stared at the emoji, then looked at George, hope filling her heart. 'Really?'

He nodded, then as though the admission had given them both wings they were in each other's arms, their mouths meeting and melding with perfect synchronicity. She kissed him with all the love in her heart, wanting him to feel just how wonderful he made her feel. In return, she felt his own need, his desire and his acceptance of their mutual love.

When one of her neighbours came out into the corridor, seeing the two of them kissing, Melody belatedly realised where they were. She'd been so caught up in everything about him that she hadn't even opened the door to her apartment. She quickly unlocked her door and beckoned him inside. It was then she realised that he, too, had a bag beside him—a large bag.

'You're staying in Sydney?'

'I'm staying wherever you are,' he told her as he gathered her close again, kicking the door shut to the apartment to ensure they had all the privacy they needed.

'I was going to do the same thing. I told Ethan I wanted to be wherever you were and that if you didn't love me I would give you all the time you needed to come to the sane and rational conclusion that we belong together.'

'You were going to leave Sydney?'

'I got a call from the CEO—they've found a new head of department so I'm free, George. I'm free to move to Melbourne or to Timbuktu—I don't care, so long as I'm with *you*.' She pressed a kiss to his lips then shook her head. 'I know we only had one week together but these past ten weeks apart have been absolute torture.' She kissed him again. 'I missed being able to talk to you, to share things with you, to just sit and spend time with you.'

'You could have called me,' he ventured, but she shook her head.

'I knew I had to be patient and to trust you, two things I needed to have more practice with.' She broke free from him for a moment and took his hand, leading him over to the lounge, where they sat down together. 'You needed to sort things out in your own way, in your own time.'

'When I returned to Melbourne—' George stopped and shook his head. 'It was as though I was having an out-of-body experience. I could walk around my house, the place I'd lived with Veronique, and it was as though I was intruding on someone else's life. It wasn't mine. It wasn't where I belonged any more. I felt the same way at the hospital. I did a few shifts over Christmas and New Year, and although everything was familiar it was…out of balance with the man I'd become.'

George shook his head and held her hands in his. 'I'm not the same man I used to be and that's all because of you, Melody.' He held her gaze as he spoke, his tone intense and filled with repressed desire. 'Our week together helped me realise that I'd merely been existing, going through my days one at a time but not really taking anything in. In the beginning the travelling had been good for my grief but it wasn't until I arrived back in Melbourne that I realised I was done.'

'Done with grieving?'

He shook his head. 'Done with the guilt from wanting to move forward.'

'Good, because I don't think you're ever *done* with grieving. It just…changes.'

'It does, and Veronique's mother told me herself that Veronique wouldn't be happy if I was always looking backwards. My wife would want me to be happy and you…' He lifted her hands to his lips and pressed soft kisses to her knuckles. 'You make me happy, Melody. Being with you, laughing with you, working with you.'

'Working with me?'

George gave her a lopsided smile and shrugged one shoulder. 'Didn't you mention St Aloysius had found a new head of the department? That you were now free to do whatever you wanted?'

Melody frowned at him for a moment before dawning realisation crossed her face. '*You're* the new head of department?'

'There was nothing for me in Melbourne any more and everything here in Sydney because Sydney is where *you* are.'

'You took the head of department position?' She laughed with rising incredulity.

'Is that OK?'

'Uh…yeah.' She nodded her head for emphasis. 'Of course it is, but are you sure you'll be happy here?'

'Yes. I like the hospital. I like Rick, who I've insisted remain as my PA, and I like the resident orthopaedic surgeon…very much.' He leaned forward as he said the last few words then captured her lips with his. 'Very much,' he reiterated a few moments later after delighting in the way Melody kissed him back with such uninhibited abandon.

'I love you, George.'

'I love you, too, Melody.'

'You do?' She smiled as though she was still unable to believe it.

'I do, so very much. My life was…incomplete without you.'

'Mine, too.'

'Then be with me for ever, Melody. You complete me and I want to feel like that for ever. Marry me?'

She gasped at his words but before she could answer, he continued.

'Let me show you I'm not like the other dead-heads who broke your heart. I love your intellect, the way we can talk about operating techniques, share the highs and the lows of our jobs. I've never had that with anyone before but when I found it with you it was as though a part of me became complete. Then another part and then another. Be my wife,' he urged. 'Complete me.'

'And children?' she asked hesitantly. 'Do you want children?'

'With you? Absolutely.' His kissed her once more, a kiss that was filled with passion and promise—the promise of a long and devoted life together. 'Say yes,' he ground out as he nibbled his way to her ear lobe. 'Say yes.'

'I will.' She laughed, happier than she'd ever been in her life. 'If you'd give me half a chance.' Goose-bumps shivered down her body as he continued his assault. Giggling, she planted her hand in his hair and gently tugged his head away. 'George!'

'Sorry. It's been so long since I've been able to kiss you like this and all I've dreamed about every day we were apart.'

'Well, we're not apart now.' Her words were filled with love, love for the man who was her soul mate, her other half. 'I'll agree to complete you if you complete me. George, you don't need to show or prove anything to me—because you've already done it. I'm not talking about moving to Sydney but the fact that you accept me just as I am. No man has ever done that before. You're the first—and the last.' She brushed her lips across his. 'Marry me quickly.'

'As you wish.' His mouth met hers in a mutual declaration of love, one they were both willing to contribute to and work at. 'How am I going to be able to keep my hands off you?' he groaned as he buried his face in her neck, unable to resist kissing the soft skin. 'Working with you every day. Sitting next to you in departmental meetings. I don't know if my self-control can take it.'

George raised his head to look at the woman he loved. The woman who had made him the happiest man on the face of the earth. He smiled at her.

'I guess we'd better work out some...' she paused and raised her eyebrows suggestively '...guidelines, then.'

His gaze darkened with desire. 'I look forward to it, Dr Janeway.'

'So do I, Professor!'

EPILOGUE

THE FOLLOWING CHRISTMAS neither George nor Melody was working. Both of them were enjoying spending their holidays with family. Ethan and CJ had decided to host Christmas at their place in Pridham, and with Melody's parents and brother Dave and his family coming to join in the festivities it was most definitely a madcap time for all of them. Donna and her husband Philip were there as well, allowing George to catch up with his old friends.

After they'd all enjoyed a huge barbeque lunch with a plethora of salads, the Australian heat giving them a slight reprieve and only being mildly hot instead of stinking hot, Melody had adjourned inside to relax in the air-conditioning. Sitting in CJ's living room, she put her feet up on the lounge and closed her eyes, a possessive hand on her slightly swollen abdomen.

'Ah, good. I was just coming to see if you were resting,' George stated as he brought her a glass of iced water.

'I am.' Just then she felt the baby move and although she'd been able to feel it shift around for a while, George was yet to feel it. 'Here. Quick.' She reached for his hand and placed it on her abdomen. 'Wait. Just wait a second.'

They both waited, their wedding rings touching as Melody placed her hand over George's. Their wedding day had been a lovely one, nice and quiet but filled with their friends and family beneath a small marquee in one of Sydney's prettiest parks. After the pomp and ceremony of the VOS, neither of them had wanted a lavish affair, preferring to focus on the main aspect, which was the two of them making an open and honest declaration of their love for each other.

Then, only two months later, Melody had announced to her husband that she thought she might be pregnant. George had instantly bought a pregnancy test and they'd waited and watched together as the test had confirmed that Melody's supposition had been correct.

A moment later the baby moved and George's eyes widened in delighted astonishment.

'Did you feel it?'

'I felt it.' He grinned widely and bent down to kiss her abdomen.

'What are you two doing?' CJ asked as she came into the room, Ethan hard on her heels, twenty-month-old Lizzie-Jean wriggling around in her daddy's arms.

'I just felt the baby kick!' George laughed. 'It's the first time.'

'It's a great feeling,' Ethan remarked, coming to stand next to his wife and placing a possessive hand on CJ's very flat stomach. 'And one we're looking forward to enjoying in a few months' time as well.'

'Wait. What?' Melody tried to sit up but found it difficult to move quickly. Thankfully, George was by her side and immediately helped her up. 'You're going to have another baby?'

'Lizzie-Jean's going to have a little brother or sister,' CJ confirmed, and the two women embraced. George and Ethan shook hands then gave each other a brotherly hug.

'We really are becoming one *big* happy family,' Melody stated, and Ethan agreed.

'Come on, CJ. Let's go and break the news to Mum and Dad that they're going to be grandparents again.'

After they'd headed out, George sat on the lounge, his

wife in his arms. 'Can you believe it? It's good that all the cousins are going to be close in age.'

'It is.' Melody smiled, tears of happiness starting to prick behind her eyes. 'It's wonderful. Where I thought I'd never find true love, never find the right man for me, into my life you came with a twinkling grin and turned my world upside down.' She kissed her husband. 'Thank you for making me so happy.'

'Right back at you,' he replied, and kissed her soundly, so glad he'd had the courage to take this second chance at love, because now his cup really did runneth over.

* * * * *

MILLS & BOON

Coming next month

REUNITED BY THEIR SECRET SON
Louisa George

Finn walked through to the waiting room and was just about to call out the boy's name when he was struck completely dumb. His heart thudded against his ribcage as he watched the woman reading a story to her child. Her voice quiet and sing-song, dark hair tumbling over one shoulder, ivory skin. A gentle manner. Soft.

His brain rewound, flickering like an old film reel: dark curls on the pillow. Warm caramel eyes. A mouth that tasted so sweet. Laughter in the face of grief. One night.

That night…

A lifetime ago.

He snapped back to reality. He wasn't that man any more; he'd do well to remember that. He cleared his throat and glanced down at the notes file in his hand to remind himself of the name. 'Lachlan Harding?'

She froze, completely taken aback. For a second he saw fear flicker across her eyes then she stood up. The fear gone, she smiled hesitantly and tugged the boy closer to her leg, her voice a little wobbly and a little less soft. 'Wow. Finn, this is a surprise—'

'Sophie. Hello. Yes, I'm Finn. Long time, no see.' Glib, he knew, when there was so much he should say to explain what had happened, why he hadn't called, but telling her his excuses during a professional consultation wasn't the right time. Besides, she had a child now; she'd moved on from their one night together, clearly. He glanced at her left hand, the one that held her boy so close—no wedding ring. But that didn't mean a thing these days; she could be happily unmarried and in a relationship.

And why her marital status pinged into his head he just didn't know. He had no right to wonder after the silence he'd held for well over two years.

They were just two people who'd shared one night a long time ago.

Continue reading
REUNITED BY THEIR SECRET SON
Louisa George

Available next month
www.millsandboon.co.uk

LET'S TALK

Romance

For exclusive extracts, competitions
and special offers, find us online:

f facebook.com/millsandboon

◎ @millsandboonuk

𝕏 @millsandboon

Or get in touch on 0844 844 1351*

For all the latest titles coming soon, visit
millsandboon.co.uk/nextmonth